# Tarantula and the Red Chigger

# TARANTULA
## and
# the Red Chigger

### by
### Mary Elsie Robertson

Little, Brown and Company
Boston                    Toronto

COPYRIGHT © 1980 BY MARY ELSIE ROBERTSON

FIRST EDITION

LIBRARY OF CONGRESS CATALOGING IN PUBLICATION DATA

Robinson, Mary Elsie.
   Tarantula and the Red Chigger.

   SUMMARY:   Ben and Lonnie, age 10, under the aliases
of Tarantula and the Red Chigger, take on the local
bullies and become friends in the process.
   [1.   Friendship—Fiction.   2.   Arkansas—Fiction]
I.   Title.
PZ7.R56752Tar      [Fic]        80-17487
ISBN 0-316-75115-4

BP

*Published simultaneously in Canada
by Little, Brown & Company (Canada) Limited*

PRINTED IN THE UNITED STATES OF AMERICA

For my son, Piers Marchant,
and for my father, Thomas Winfield Robertson

# Tarantula and the Red Chigger

# Chapter

## 1

I didn't want to go to Grandma's house again this summer. I had the feeling this August wasn't going to be like all the other Augusts we'd spent in Arkansas. And when I got there I found I was right.

Other summers, as soon as we passed through Sherburn and started down the road that led to Grandma's house, my brother Ned and I would start pointing out things we remembered. "The blue house!" we'd shout. "And the wagon-wheel gate! Mr. Park's goats!" Then a long stretch of nothing much, just fields and pastures before we came to the woods and the bumpy trail that led to the Lesters' house. From there we could see the big trees in Grandma's yard, and the mailbox and even the chimney and the dark grey roof of the house. If it had been any other summer I'd have started shouting, "I see it! I see it!"

when Mom and I got that far, but this time I didn't feel like it.

It wasn't any fun to shout without Ned along. Ned's my brother, he's fourteen, and he didn't go to Arkansas because he went to summer camp — this place called Muskokegan Camp in the Berkshires. He hadn't been to camp before, though Toby and John, his best friends, had. And that's the main reason that I knew I wasn't going to have much fun at Grandma's. I wouldn't have Ned to do things with.

I don't know why he had to go to that camp. You couldn't even tell from his letters if he liked it or not. "Took the canoes across the lake on Wed.," he wrote in his last letter. "Stayed on an island and came back on Sun. It was OK. Couldn't sleep though because of the frogs." What can you tell from that? You can't tell if the frogs kept them awake by jumping on them or because they croaked or what. They must've done something for five days besides listen to frogs. I thought they must've brainwashed Ned, somehow, at that camp and wouldn't let him write about what was really going on, but Mom said no. Ned was just trying to act grown up.

So, anyway, Ned's at that camp listening to frogs, or whatever he's doing, and Dad didn't come to Arkansas this year either because he's going to this institute in California that his company is sending him to. So it was just Mom and me. We drove all the way from Tarrytown, New York, where we live, and

I felt kind of lonesome even before we got to Grandma's house.

Mom turned in the driveway that runs between the two long rows of crape myrtle bushes and parked the car under the walnut tree, same as always. We were nearly to the steps before Grandma heard us and got to the door. She hugged me the same as always and said to my mother, "Why, Margaret, you made it after all, and look at Ben, would you now! Haven't got a baby in the family anymore, have we?"

Of course I haven't been a baby for a long time — I'm eleven now — but I'm used to Grandma saying that.

I measured myself against Grandma the way I always do. When I stood very straight my head nearly touched her chin. "Next year I'll bet I'm as tall as you are, Grandma," I said. Grandma isn't very tall; she says she's short because she's worn her legs down with all the work she's done in her life, and maybe she has, because she hardly ever sits down. She's always doing something, even if it's just watering geraniums.

The house smelled the same as ever. Gingerbread. When I was four or five, gingerbread was my very favorite thing to eat, so Grandma always has a pan of it waiting for me when I come in the door, although, to tell the truth, I'm not as crazy about gingerbread as I used to be.

I went out to the kitchen and had a big piece

anyway with milk so I wouldn't hurt Grandma's feelings. I even had a second piece to be polite, but Mom and Grandma were so busy talking I doubt if they noticed.

After I finished eating I went out to the car to get my suitcase, and I took it upstairs to the room Ned and I had always shared before. The windows there look out over the back fields, the pond, and the woods. It had been Uncle Warren's room when he was a boy. His model airplanes are still there, swinging on strings from the ceiling. The planes look almost like they're flying in a breeze. They're the kind you make with thin strips of balsa wood and glue and tissue paper. Very light. I don't know anybody who makes that kind of airplane anymore. The B29 Liberator is my favorite and I gave it a little flip when I walked by.

Grandma's good about keeping things. Not like Mom, who throws out stuff right and left. When I opened the closet door, there were all the things that Ned and I leave each year in Arkansas — the kites we made once, a baseball bat, ball, and two gloves, a pair of stilts we made last summer, a soccer ball with the air out of it. She even had saved some trucks from when we were really little, but there wasn't a thing there that I felt like playing with by myself.

I put my clothes in the bottom drawer of the bureau but I left my comics in the bottom of my suitcase. I brought along the best ones in my collection because I was afraid the house might burn down while I was away, and I wouldn't be there to save them. Here, if the house catches on fire I'll remember to grab them before I climb out the window. I brought along my Hulks, one through five; Spiderman, numbers three and four; Daredevils, two, four, five, seven, eight, nine, ten; and the Fantastic Four, six through fourteen. Before I came down here to Grandma's I left all the money I had — four dollars — with my friend Richard so he could buy me the current ones. I wasn't sure which comics they'd have here.

After that, I sat on the bed because I couldn't think of anything else to do. I'd been at Grandma's for less than an hour and already I couldn't think of anything to do. Boy. One hour down and just a month to go. I wished I were at home where I could go over to Richard's house and see if he'd gotten any new comics, or we could go swimming or get together with some other kids and play soccer. Or *something*.

I knew that I couldn't sit there on the bed for the next month, so I dug my favorite G.I. Joe, Bernie, out of the little drawstring bag of toys I'd brought along and went outside. I thought that I might as well check on the tree house that Ned and Dad and I had built last summer in the big oak tree down by the pond.

It was hot. It's always hot in Arkansas in the summertime. If Mom had seen me she'd have called for me to put on a hat, but she didn't see me. I cut through the barn lot and headed for the pond. The lot was grown up with weeds pretty bad, so I picked up a long stick to thump ahead of me in case of snakes. I was glad to get to the oak tree and climb up to the tree house where a snake wasn't likely to get me.

It's a really good tree house, with a wide platform and walls on three sides and even a roof over half of it. But even the greatest tree house in the world isn't too much fun if you have to play in it by yourself.

I did my best, playing with Bernie, pretending we were on a boat going through shark-infested seas, low on food and water and no land in sight. There was also a very bad robot monster after us, sent by some evil genius who could tune in on everything going on in the world on a little screen no bigger than a plate. I was the Tarantula, which is my secret superhero identity, and I was about to find this evil genius in his laboratory.

A tarantula is a kind of giant, hairy spider that can jump three or four feet at one bound. When I was being Tarantula I pretended I could jump as high as a building, and a bite from me would paralyze a criminal.

I was just getting into this story, doing all the talking for me and Bernie and even the mad genius and the robot monster, when I got a funny feeling that somebody was watching me.

I looked all around, at the pond and the barn

and the fields and the woods, and then, sure enough, standing just at the edge of the woods was Lonnie Lester, the pest. He always hangs around in the summers when Ned and I are here. The Lesters live in the house closest to Grandma's, even though it's three-quarters of a mile away and back in the woods where you can't see it from the road. They all live there in a tumbledown house leaning to one side, with three old cars without any tires rusting away in the back-yard. Ned and I used to get very fed up with Lonnie just standing around watching us; that's why we called him the pest. When we'd yell at him to bug off, he'd throw rocks at us.

So there the pest stood, wearing shorts and a skimpy tee-shirt that pulled up tight under his arms, scratching on one arm and whistling through his teeth. He'd grown some in the year, but not much.

He swatted the gnats away from his face and started walking over to my tree, coming right on through the weeds without even looking down for snakes.

At the foot of the tree he stopped and looked up.

"How come you're up there by yourself?" he said, craning his neck to look up. He was kind of a scrawny kid with ears that stuck out a little bit.

That was about the dumbest question I ever heard. "What's it look like?" I said.

"Where's your brother, then?"

"Summer camp."

He stood down at the bottom of the tree, and I stood leaning over the rail looking down at him. We could have stood like that for quite a while.

"I been up there," he said finally, looking up at me with eyes that were a little bit too blue and a little bit too wide to suit me. I know this boy, Roger, at home, and every time he starts telling something that's just made up with not a word of truth in it, he opens his eyes just like that. "Last summer when you all left, I spent a whole night up there. Took me a blanket and all. Woke up next morning and there was this big tarantula, big as my hand about, sitting right there in front of my nose."

"Tarantulas hardly ever get that big," I said.

"You ever see a tarantula up close?"

I shook my head.

"He had these little bitty red eyes and a kind of shiny place in the middle of his back." While he talked Lonnie climbed the ladder to the tree house, and when he got to the top he started walking around like he owned the place.

"Well, did he bite you?" I asked.

"Naw. He just looked at me a little while and I looked back at him, and then he went jumping off. Tarantulas can jump five feet when they've a mind to, but this one was just taking little hops along."

"When my friend Richard and I play super-heroes at home that's what I am, the Tarantula," I said. "That's my secret identity." As soon as I said it, I wished I hadn't. A secret identity is supposed to be *secret*.

Lonnie pulled a leaf off the tree and started chewing on the stem. "What's Richard, then?" he asked after a minute.

"The Cobra."

"Could I have a secret name like that too?"

"It's a free country," I said, wishing I hadn't even mentioned secret identities.

"Well, but what could I be?"

"Anything. Something dangerous or sneaky."

"OK," Lonnie said. "I'll be the Red Chigger."

I thought maybe he was making a joke, but he didn't look like he was. "But that's silly, Lonnie. What's dangerous about a chigger? They're such little things."

"The way they bite. And there's nothing sneakier. They can get in anywhere and you can't even see them. They can make you itch all summer. Tarantulas aren't dangerous, you know, come to that. They just look mean."

"All right, *be* the Red Chigger," I said. I didn't really care. Lonnie didn't know how to play the game anyway.

"How old are you?" Lonnie asked, having gotten the Red Chigger thing settled.

"Eleven."

"Hey, so'm I! When's your birthday?"

"Sixth of February."

"Mine's the seventh!"

"What grade'll you be in?"

"Sixth."

"So will I."

"You ever break your arm?"

"No," I said. "I had pneumonia once, though."

"Shoot, I've broke this arm twice and my big toe once, and I had to have five stitches in my head once where I ran into this big piece of sheet iron."

"My dad rides a motorcycle down to catch the train every morning," I said, thinking hard.

"My daddy's a water witch," Lonnie said.

"What's that?" I had this picture in my mind of a witch wearing a long, black cape thing floating along on the water.

"Don't you even know what that is? He can find out where water is under the ground. There's this witchin' rod, and he walks around all over the ground, and when he gets to where there's water, the witchin' rod goes down. Can't even hold it up if you put all your weight behind it. Just like a hand pulling it down to the ground."

"I don't think there is anything like that," I said. I knew for sure we hadn't studied anything like that in science class.

"Come on home with me and I'll show you," Lonnie said, jumping up.

Well, I had to see this thing. I owed it to my

science class next year. So we went over to Lonnie's house. I'd seen it before when Ned and I cut through the woods to go somewhere, and it didn't look any better than I remembered, the whole thing kind of leaning to one side on the spindly piles of rocks at the corners. A big dog came from under the back porch shaking dirt off his fur. He looked like he had some hound in him and some Labrador and something like Great Dane. He was big, anyway, mostly black with brown ears and chest.

"That's just Geronimo," Lonnie said. "He won't bite you. He won't do nothing but eat and lie in a cool place."

When I held out my hand Geronimo came up and sniffed it. I like medium-sized dogs better than big ones.

Lonnie's dad, a tall, skinny man, was in the garden running a hand plow down the rows. He waved to us once and went on with his plowing. He didn't look like a witch to me.

Lonnie went to the back porch and came back with a forked stick in his hand. "You mean that's *it?*" I said. "The thing for finding water?"

"Sure. It's a green one. Has to be green. Willow trees are the best. Then you just walk around with it like this."

He held the two forks in his hands and walked around with the straight piece in front of him. I walked along behind him but I didn't see anything happening, and it was hot and the bites the chiggers had given me on the legs as I went through the weeds were starting to itch.

We walked all the way around the house and nothing happened. So I asked Lonnie to let me try it, and I walked all around the house again, holding the stick out in front of me and feeling a little silly.

"I didn't think it would work," I said, handing it back to Lonnie. "I mean, it would be in all the science books, wouldn't it, if that was the way to find out where water was?"

Then Lonnie's dad came over to us, taking the straw hat off his head to let the breeze in.

"Ben doesn't think water witchin' works," Lonnie said.

"Well, up where he comes from I don't guess they go in for water witchin'," Lonnie's dad said. Of course he knew who I was; country people always know things like that. He took the stick from me and somehow, as soon as he took it in his hands, it had a different look about it. He held it so the end was pointing up to the sky, but it wasn't just that. He started walking slowly, balancing the forked pieces of the stick between his hands, and when we'd gotten to the edge of the porch, that stick began to twitch. I saw it. And then he took two more steps and that stick pointed straight down to the ground like an arrow.

"You'd get yourself a real good well if you dug there," he said. "Good strong stream."

Of course I thought he'd just done it himself, just letting the stick point down himself, and I wasn't impressed or anything. But then he motioned for me to come over, and he put the stick in my hands and closed them over the ends of the stick.

"Now just walk slow and easy, the way I did," he said, going along right beside me, and, I don't know, but that stick felt different to me this time. Like there was an electric current going through it or something like that. I walked just where he'd walked before, and when I got close to that place by the porch, the stick started moving in my hands. It was the strangest thing!

"See if you can hold it straight," Lonnie's dad said. And I did try but I couldn't do it. No matter how hard I held on, that stick just went down toward the ground. It must've been like fishing and getting a great big fish on the end of your line.

"See?" Lonnie said. "You believe me now? I told you it worked."

"I don't know," I said. "I just don't see how . . ."

Lonnie's dad laughed and told me I'd make a fine water witch if I wanted to turn my hand to it one day. That some had the gift and some didn't. He gave me the stick to keep, although he said it worked better with a fresh green one every time. I couldn't wait to show Ned and Richard and maybe all the kids in my class that I was a witch.

I was just putting my stick in a safe place on the porch when I felt something tug on my britches leg, and I looked down to see this little kid — baby, practically — hanging on to my leg. It was a girl with curly blond hair and not wearing a thing but a diaper, and the diaper was drooping so it looked like she was about to lose it. When she saw me looking at her she smiled a big smile and said, "Hibo, hibo."

"Hi," I said, not very enthusiastically. I like puppies and kittens but I'm not crazy about human babies.

"That's my little baby sister," Lonnie said. "Her name's Sylvie. She wants you to pick her up."

"What's she saying?"

"Hi, boy. She just learned that. Didn't you, Sylvie, you little dumpling?"

Sylvie giggled at Lonnie but she went on hanging on to my jeans.

"She really likes you," Lonnie said. "She wants you to pick her up and give her a big hug."

I couldn't see any way out of it. I leaned over and put my hands under Sylvie's arms and lifted. But, boy, she was heavier than she looked. I kind of staggered back and Sylvie put her legs around my waist and hung on like a monkey. When she did that I knew why her diaper had looked so droopy.

"Hey, Lonnie," I said weakly, "I think your little sister's wet."

"That Sylvie's always wet," he said. "We better take her in to Momma."

I thought maybe he'd take her and carry her himself, but no such luck. He acted like it was some kind of privilege to carry his wet, heavy little sister, and she didn't show any signs of wanting to turn loose of me either. In fact, when I finally staggered up the steps and into the kitchen where Lonnie's mother was sitting at the table peeling potatoes, Sylvie didn't want to let go at all. Her mother had to pull her off while she tried to hang on like an octopus. She was yelling bloody murder when she finally had to let go and was carried off to get her diaper changed. My shirt felt all wet and clammy where she'd been against me but nobody took any notice. I shook out my shirt and hoped it would dry.

"You hungry?" Lonnie said, reaching into the pan where his mother had been cutting up potatoes and handing me one of the raw pieces.

I'd never eaten a piece of raw potato in my life, since the only way I like potatoes is French fried. I wasn't even sure that raw potato would be good for a person, but when Lonnie sprinkled salt on both pieces and gave me one I took a bite.

It tasted kind of weird, but not as bad as I thought it would. In fact it wasn't much worse than cooked potato. And if it gave me a stomach ache, my mother couldn't say anything. She's always after me to try new things.

"Lonnie!" his mother called out from the room where she'd carried Sylvie. "Go get me some more potatoes. I'm just about out."

Lonnie groaned. "I can't *stand* getting potatoes," he said to me under his breath. "I'm always the one has to do it."

"I know what you mean," I said. "At home I'm always the one who has to carry out the garbage."

"Shoot, I wouldn't mind that too bad. But *potatoes!*" He picked up the empty paper sack and motioned for me to come along. I supposed the potatoes were in some big sack in the pantry, which is where Grandma keeps hers, and I couldn't see what Lonnie was making such a fuss about, but no, he took me outside and started crawling under the house.

"What're you going under there for?"

"For potatoes! They keep cool under here."

I started crawling along behind him and I saw why getting the potatoes was so bad. We had to crawl on our hands and knees and I was afraid Geronimo would come and get me when I couldn't even run or anything. But Geronimo didn't seem to be around. He must've found himself another cool place.

We kept running into spiderwebs, and I *hate*

that prickly feeling of spiderweb on my face. And it was kind of spooky under there. Vines and weeds and things grew along the edges of the house so it was dim and it smelled musty like cool, damp dirt does.

I was just plodding along behind Lonnie feeling like some big turtle when all of a sudden he snapped backward and drew in his breath.

"What is it?" I whispered. I knew by the way he was acting that it must be something terrible.

He didn't say anything. He just inched back against my shoulder, not taking his eyes from some spot ahead and to our right. I raised my head a little to see over his shoulder and looked where I thought he was looking. At first I couldn't see anything. There was a little dip in the ground with a potato or two lying at the edge of it, and at first it just looked shadowy in there. But then something happened that made the goose bumps break out all over me. The darkness in that dip in the ground seemed to rise a little and then sink down. I stared so, I could feel my eyes getting big like a cat's. And then suddenly all the light and dark fell into place, and I saw.

A snake was lying looped around on top of the potatoes, and it had lifted its head to look at us.

"Oh, boy," I said, just barely breathing out the words. "Oh, boy." I went cold all over. If I'd been out in the open I'd have run like crazy, but under there I could hardly move at all. We both froze like rabbits in a car's headlights.

The snake saw us, all right. He had his head lifted and his tongue was going in and out. He was maybe ten feet away, and there were so many loops of snake heaving a little on top of the potatoes that I couldn't even guess how long he would be stretched out. He was mottled, though, I could tell, and I knew what that meant. He lifted his stubby, mean-looking head a little higher, moving it back and forth so he could focus on us, and I thought maybe he was getting ready to coil. I could hear a hum, a whirring kind of sound that I knew had to be his rattle; I hadn't gone to all those nature lectures at the museum on Saturday mornings for nothing.

"Go backward," Lonnie whispered. He sounded funny, like somebody whose mouth is still numb after getting a tooth filled.

So I inched my way backward, feeling my way with the toes of my sneakers. Lonnie moved every time I did. We were as close together as Siamese twins. We didn't dare turn our heads. We just kept our eyes right on that snake. He kept his on us too. Nothing changed until we backed out so far that I could feel sunlight on my britches legs. Then the snake lowered its head and it looked like something flowed along the ground at that end of the house.

Suddenly we were in the open and running for the garden where Lonnie's dad was working.

"There's a great big rattlesnake under the house," Lonnie shouted, and his dad took his hoe and ran in that direction. All we did was fall down in the row between the tomato plants and sit there with our legs hunched. It was funny, but even though we were right out in the sun the goose pimples stayed on our arms, and our teeth started chattering like we were about to freeze to death.

I looked over at Lonnie and he looked terrible, with his hair sticking up and dirt on his knees, and his face as white as mine when I'm about to throw up from getting carsick. But he didn't look like the pest anymore.

"I sure thought we were goners," Lonnie said.

"I did too."

"It's funny, but things like that are always happening to me."

I should have taken warning right there when he said that, but I didn't. "I guess the Tarantula and the Red Chigger won out again," I said.

"Hey, we did, didn't we?"

"Sure."

It felt so good to be out from under that house I didn't even mind too much when Sylvie got away from Lonnie's mother and made a beeline for me. She sat down in my lap just like somebody told her she could, and I let her stay there saying, "Hibo, hibo," and patting my leg.

After a while Lonnie's father came around the house fussing because the snake had disappeared.

We had a unit in science last year about life

cycles so I knew that snakes were useful since they ate rats and mice and things, and you shouldn't kill them. But I knew, too, that I never wanted to see that snake again, ever.

After we'd recovered a little bit I said it must be close to suppertime and my mother would be worried about me. So I got my witching rod from the porch, and Lonnie walked me down to the road. Sylvie came along and I carried her since I knew Lonnie would have to carry her up again, and she wasn't any featherweight, let me tell you. It took us quite a while to get down the road because we jumped every time we saw a stick that took us by surprise.

"I'll see you tomorrow, Red Chigger," I told Lonnie when I handed Sylvie over to him. "What time do you finish breakfast?"

"We get done early. Way before you all will. I'll just come down here to the road and wait around for you."

On the way to Grandma's house I decided I wouldn't say anything about the snake. It doesn't pay to let mothers and grandmothers know everything that happens to you.

That night I wrote a letter to Ned kind of paying him back for the kind of letters he wrote us. "Dear Ned," I wrote. "How are you? We are fine. Something terrible happened to me this afternoon. I could have gotten snakebite. Well, all for now. Love, Ben."

I wrote another letter to Richard, only I called

him the Cobra, telling him the whole story, but swearing him to secrecy. On the bottom of the letter I drew a picture of Tarantula fighting off this snake that had reared up as tall as a building. It turned out to be a pretty good picture, if I say so myself.

# Chapter

## 2

The next morning I got away from Grandma's house as fast as I could, but I had to dry dishes and then I had to make my bed, so it must've been pushing nine by the time I left.

Lonnie was hunkering by their mailbox watching some ants or something. "You sure are slow," he said when I got to him. "It must be practically dinner time."

"Only nine."

"Shoot. I been here since eight."

"I couldn't help it, Lonnie. I had to do some things before they'd let me out of the house."

"Well, what do you want to do?"

"Don't ask me."

I sat down in the dirt beside him. Locusts had already started whirring. It was going to be another boiling hot day. Heat like that makes me go kind of sleepy, and I thought we might just sit there the rest of the day watching the ants scrounge around in the red dust and listening to the locusts saw up the air.

"What would you do if you was home?" Lonnie asked.

"Go swimming."

"We could go swimming here."

"Mom won't let me swim in the river or in the rock quarries. Sometimes she'll take me over to Turner's Lake, but I don't think she'd do that today."

"Aw, you don't have to go any of those places. There's a real good place along Six-Mile Creek."

"You mean wading?"

"Naw, you can swim. Not over your head, anywhere in it."

"OK. I guess my mother wouldn't mind that. I'll just have to go home and get my suit."

"What do you need a suit for? Nobody's going to see you."

"All right," I said. I knew I should go and tell Mom where I was going anyway, but it was a mile there and back and the heat was getting up. And if the water in this swimming place wasn't even over my head I couldn't see what could happen. I can do the backstroke, the crawl, and the sidestroke, and I've done emergency bobbing for twenty minutes at a time. "I have to be back by twelve-thirty. That's when they expect me for lunch," I told Lonnie.

We went by Lonnie's house and he made a

couple of peanut-butter sandwiches. We didn't take anything to drink, since I figured we could drink creek water.

We sneaked away from Lonnie's house in case Sylvie saw us leaving and set up a wail. We made it, and only Geronimo tagged along. For a little while we chased each other around, but we didn't keep it up. It was just too hot. Every time a pickup truck went by we got covered with dust, so I was glad when Lonnie took off on a path through the woods.

We kept trying to get Geronimo to go in front of us to scare away snakes, but he wouldn't do it. He'd just stand with his tongue hanging out until we'd passed him and then he'd jog along behind. I laughed at Lonnie because the red dust from the road had stuck to his face and arms and he looked like somebody had made him up to be a blond-headed Indian. He said I looked just as bad, but if I looked like an Indian, at least my hair was the right color.

Finally we came out at the creek and it was a whole lot easier going. We just waded through the water, not even bothering to take off our sneakers because of the rocks.

The creek broadened out at the swimming hole, and it was a really nice place. You could tell the water was deeper there because it was a darker color. There were big willow trees growing along the banks, and there were some big rocks where we could leave our

clothes. It didn't take us long to skin out of our clothes,
put the sandwiches on a tree branch so Geronimo
couldn't eat them, and throw a few rocks in the water
to discourage any snakes that might be lurking
around. Then we jumped in. Did it ever feel *good!*
Geronimo barked on the bank, but then he came in
too, swimming around us.

I saw I was a better swimmer than Lonnie since
all he could do was the dog paddle. It didn't matter,
since we could stand on our hands, float on our backs,
and try to pull each other under. We were making
so much noise that I guess it wasn't any wonder we
didn't hear anything until all of a sudden there was a
strange dog barking at Geronimo from the bank, and
we looked up to see two boys watching us from the
top of one of the rocks. Big boys. Bigger even than
Ned. They looked fifteen or sixteen to me. They had
baseball caps down practically to their eyes, and
cowboy boots on their feet. The taller one was wearing a blue and yellow shirt with horses rearing up on
it, and the shorter and heftier one was wearing a
cowboy jacket without a shirt. I didn't like the looks
of them.

"Who're they?" I asked Lonnie out of the corner
of my mouth, but he just shook his head and joggled
his finger back and forth, which meant, I guess, that
he would tell me later.

Their dog, which was a mean-looking blue tick

hound, was walking stiff-legged up and down the bank growling, hackles up. I felt sorry for poor old Geronimo, who was swimming around in circles so he wouldn't have to get out of the water and fight. I didn't blame him, either. *I* didn't want to tangle with those two in the baseball caps.

"Looky at those two little white turtles out there in the middle of the creek," the short one said. "Come on out of there, turtles, and let's see what you look like."

They started throwing little flat creek rocks at us and they hurt if they hit. "Duck under the water," I told Lonnie.

Lonnie just stuck his bottom jaw out in a stubborn way. "They're not getting by with *nothing*," he said. "I know those two."

I knew their kind. Ned and I once got knocked off our bicycles and had them stolen by two boys who looked a lot like those two on the bank.

"Just don't fool with them, Lonnie," I whispered to him, but I could tell he wasn't listening.

Just then the two boys found our clothes we'd left in the shade.

"Why, those two little turtles have shed their clothes right here on the rock," the tall one said. "Everybody knows turtles don't need clothes."

When they started scooping everything up, Lonnie couldn't stand it any longer. "Your brother's in jail and your grandpa eats rabbits he finds dead on the highway!" he yelled, and those two on the bank looked at us meaner than before.

"You little fleabites want to get yourselves drowned like a couple of kittens?" the short one said.

I grabbed Lonnie and ducked him under the water so he couldn't say anything more. When he came up, spluttering, those two were running into the woods with all our clothes. We could hear them back there, whooping it up and throwing our clothes all over the woods.

"I'll get 'em!" Lonnie kept saying. "I'll fix their plows!"

"They're a lot bigger than we are," I said, hanging on to him so he couldn't go rushing out of the water. "We can't fight them like this. We don't even have any clothes. Tell me who they are, anyway."

"The short one is Butchie Manning and the tall one is Leroy Manning and they're as mean as snakes. A whole lot of Mannings live up on Mulberry Mountain, and none of them're any good. Butchie and Leroy got kicked out of school for two weeks last year for putting a skunk in the girls' rest room."

The Mannings came out of the woods long enough to yell, "Hey! Turtles! You're going to have to go home to your mommas in your birthday suits because you're not never going to get those clothes back again."

"We'll get you!" Lonnie shouted. "You just wait and see."

"You and who else? What can a nekkid turtle do?"

They whistled for their dog and sauntered off. We waited a little while and then climbed out of the water and started looking for our clothes.

We found our underwear without much trouble, but we couldn't even touch it because they'd scattered it over a thick, gruesome-looking vine of poison oak. We could see Lonnie's shorts, too, but they were in the top of a big tree and we couldn't dislodge them with rocks.

This is what we found: one of my sneakers they'd left on an anthill and one of Lonnie's socks they'd dropped without noticing. So how were we going to get home two miles down a public road without any clothes on? We couldn't go back through the woods without even any shoes and we couldn't hop all that way in one shoe and one sock. Even if we did go through the woods we'd come out on the road sooner or later.

"We'll have to go through the creek to the highway," Lonnie said. "Maybe we can find old things people've left on the bank that we could wear."

Well, we found an old rusty bait bucket and quite a few beer cans, but we couldn't make pants for ourselves out of beer cans or a bait bucket.

"If they think they can get away with this they've got another think coming," Lonnie said as we sloshed through the water. "They're going to have to deal with the Tarantula and the Red Chigger. Right, Ben?"

"Sure. Right," I said without much enthusiasm.

I kept wondering how Daredevil or Iron Man would have managed something like this, but I couldn't see either one of them ever being caught without any clothes on. I wished I really could call on my Tarantula powers and go along jumping as high as the trees, but I couldn't do it. All I was doing was getting sunburned across the shoulders and being chewed on by mosquitoes. Even Geronimo just plodded along with his tail down.

"We even forgot those peanut-butter sandwiches," I said, and my stomach let out a big growl just thinking about them.

I couldn't see any way out of it. When we got to the road we were going to have to hide in the ditch when a car went by, and if we saw anybody's unguarded washing hanging out on the line we were going to have to steal it.

I was walking ahead of Lonnie and Geronimo when the creek made a wide bend, so I was the first to see the crazy man. He was down on his hands and knees in the water, and he had so much hair and beard I couldn't even see his face. He looked like a bear wearing a pair of britches. I turned around and ran back as quietly as I could, trying not to splash very much.

"Lonnie, there's a crazy man up ahead!" I said,

grabbing him by the arm. "He's got long, shaggy hair and he's crawling around in the water, scooting fast in one direction and then the other."

"Lemme see," Lonnie said. I wanted to get out of there, but, of course, there wasn't anywhere to go. So I held on to Geronimo's collar while Lonnie went up ahead to look, keeping to the edge of the creek where tree branches hid him.

Then all of a sudden he was out in the middle of the creek yelling to the crazy man and waving for me and Geronimo to come on.

The crazy man was standing up watching us when I reached Lonnie.

I hung back but Lonnie kept saying it was OK. "I know him," he said. "It's just Jesse, and he isn't any more crazy than you are."

I didn't realize until we'd nearly reached Jesse that the shadow he was standing in was from the highway bridge over the creek, so anybody passing in a car could have seen Lonnie and me running down the creek with no clothes on. But it was too late then.

Jesse came out to meet us and I saw that up close he looked all right, except his hair stood out like a brush.

"Ben thought you was a crazy man, Jesse," Lonnie said.

Jesse laughed, which sounded about like a bear laughing, and said, "Well, he sure's not the first and I don't expect he'll be the last to hold that opinion."

"What were you doing crawling around in the creek?" I asked.

"Why, son, hadn't you ever seen anybody trying to catch crawdads before? Go look in that pot over there and you'll see how lucky I've been."

There was a black pot sitting on some flat rocks with a fire to keep the water in it boiling. The crawdads in the pot looked like baby lobsters.

"Ben's not from around here," Lonnie said. "He comes from New York and I bet he's never had a crawdad to eat in his life."

I shook my head.

"Well, you're in luck today, aren't you, boys?" Jesse said. "Looks like, though, you've run into a little bit of trouble somewhere along the way this morning."

"You know Leroy and Butchie Manning from up on the Mountain?" Lonnie said.

"I've made their acquaintance. They're the ones kept emptying off my trotline until I caught 'em redhanded."

"They took our clothes!" Lonnie said. "Ever stitch. Threw 'em all around in the trees and on top of poison oak."

"Well, you can't go home to your mommas like that, can you now? You might as well stay and eat dinner, and I'll see if I can find something to cover your hides with."

There was an old black van parked right under

the bridge so people driving by on the highway would never know that it was there. The van had Summit Farm Eggs written on the side. The chickens painted at each end of the words looked at them as though they were thinking about pecking them. The whole picture was faded though, so it wasn't too noticeable. Jesse opened the back of the van and started poking around and talking to himself. When he came out again he had two pairs of khaki trousers in his hands that he threw to us to put on.

We didn't have to unbutton them or anything. All we had to do was step into them. The trouble was trying to keep them up once they were on. We rolled the legs up and then held on to the tops with both hands. It wasn't too bad if we didn't try to move.

"May not look like much, but it's better than nothing," Jesse said. "Sit yourselves on down and I'll see what I can find you to eat."

I was so hungry I had to hold my breath to keep my stomach from growling. We squatted on our haunches and waited for him to give us plates. We had a while to wait, because he started fixing something else to eat to go with the crawdads. He stuck an iron skillet on the rocks above the fire to get hot and proceeded to mix up some cornmeal and water and egg.

"Do you do all your cooking over the fire like that?" I asked.

"Don't see any kitchen around anyplace, do you,

son? You're sitting right now in my bedroom and kitchen and parlor rolled into one."

He did have everything he needed right there under the bridge: a cot sitting beside the van, a card table and a chair, a couple of plastic buckets down by the creek for hauling water. Inside the back of the van his cooking pots hung on hooks, and there were a couple of wooden boxes built along the sides to hold everything else he needed.

"Do you live here all the time?" I asked.

"Just in the summers, son. When bad weather sets in I have to go back to Oklahoma City and live with my daughter. Got my own little apartment in the basement of her house. Everything I'm supposed to need, but, son, a wintertime of looking out at other people's backyards is enough for me. Come warm weather and I'm off like a shot. Free as the wind living under here. Little fishing when I feel like it. Sleeping all day if I want to. Nothing to do except what I feel like doing."

Jesse poured a little of the batter he'd mixed up onto the hot skillet and made a cornmeal pancake. "Hoecake," Jesse said. "I don't expect you've had that before either."

When it was done he put it on one of the rocks, fished a couple of crawdads out of the water, put them on the hoecake, and handed the whole thing to Lonnie.

I watched Lonnie break open the crawdad shell

and pick out the meat with his fingers, so when Jesse handed me mine I knew how to go about eating it.

Crawdads taste pretty good. A little bit like lobster but tangier.

We gave little pieces of hoecake to Geronimo to keep him content, and we all ate what Jesse called a big bait of crawdads. Afterward all we had to do was lick our fingers. Not a dish to wash.

"I think when I grow up I'll live like this myself," I said. I was just about to go to sleep — it was the long hot part of the afternoon when you have a hard time keeping your eyes open — but a sudden terrible thought made me sit straight up.

"What time is it?" I asked, kind of frantic.

"I leave my watch in Oklahoma City all summer," Jesse said, "but judging by the sun I'd say it was about one-thirty, give or take a little."

"Oh, boy!" I said. "My mother'll kill me. I was supposed to be back at twelve-thirty to eat. She'll have a fit."

"Well, pile in the truck, boys, and I'll get you home," Jesse said.

Geronimo had to ride with us too, so it was pretty crowded, but I had worse things to think about.

They dropped me off and went on toward Lonnie's. I knew it was going to be bad when I got back, but when I first came into the house carrying one shoe in my hand and holding up Jesse's britches, both Mom and Grandma rushed into the hallway calling out in a relieved way, "Here he is." At first they were glad to see me, but in a few minutes, after they saw I was all right, they started getting mad.

I hadn't told Mom where I was going that morning, which was offense number one, and I hadn't gotten home when I was supposed to, which was offense number two. Also, Mom was mad about my clothes, although I played down that whole thing and pretended that the Manning boys had hidden our clothes as a joke. Which wasn't exactly true.

Grandma took up for me and said she'd heard tales about what troublemakers the Manning boys were, and she knew all about Jesse under the bridge and knew he was "a harmless old codger." She said she'd make a big batch of chocolate-chip cookies to take back with the trousers.

To make a long story short, Mom said I needed to learn not to break the rules, so I wasn't allowed to play with Lonnie for two days, and one of those was a Sunday when I had to dress up and go to church. Things didn't get back to being endurable again until Monday morning when I found a note from Lonnie in the mailbox.

# Chapter

## 3

The note said, *Meet me in the tree house soon's you can.*

R.C.

I thought it was pretty smart of Lonnie to ask me to come to the tree house because even if my mother were still mad, she wouldn't care if I went down there. Anyway, Mom and Grandma were up to their elbows in sweet corn that they were canning in the kitchen, so I didn't have any trouble getting away.

When I got to the tree house Lonnie was lying on his back squinting up at the leaves. He went on doing that even after I said hi.

"I been thinking," he said.

"You don't have to call me down here every time you get a thought, do you?"

"Just thinking about *it*," he said. "This plan I got for getting back at Leroy and Butchie." He sat up and looked at me the way he'd been looking at the leaves. A little dopey.

"I think I got it worked out because, see, there's one thing I know about Leroy and Butchie that no-body else knows."

"What's that?"

"They set out traps on the army land, and I even think I know where. You know about the army camp land?"

Sure, I knew. National Guard units came there in the summers and made such a noise that it sounded sometimes like a real war was taking place. Naturally all that land was thick with _No Trespassing Order of the U.S. Government_ signs. If the Mannings were going in there to set traps they were breaking the law.

"What makes you think so?"

"I found out about the traps because the Mannings ride the same school bus I do, and I've heard them talking in the back. And I'm pretty sure I know where the traps are because of something last fall. I was in the camp myself getting pears from this little bunch of pear trees I know about. While I was filling up my hat with pears I saw Leroy and Butchie cutting down from the road to a strip of woods along Six-Mile. Same creek we went swimming in, only higher up. They went straight in and came out five minutes later with a dead rabbit. Not even a shot. So they must've caught it in a trap."

"OK," I said. "Supposing you're right about the traps and supposing we can find them. What then?"

"Why, we spring them! And they won't know it's us or even anything human because we'll brush away any tracks we make so it'll look to them like a haint or something like that is springing their traps all the time."

That part kind of appealed to me. It would be a little bit like having a secret identity, and I always did think one of the best things about being a superhero would be the disguise — most of the time looking like anybody else until *whammo!* you take off your ordinary clothes and there are your superhero things underneath.

"What'll the soldiers do to us if they catch us trespassing?"

"We'll say we got lost."

The more I thought about the plan the better I liked it. "Great!" I said, jumping up. "Let's go get started."

"Hold your horses. This is going to take us a while, and your momma's going to carry on if you're not home to eat dinner. So let's meet here again as soon as we eat and go then."

Which is what we did.

I didn't have any trouble whatsoever in getting away from the house because Mom and Grandma went to visit some old friend of Grandma's and all Mom said was for me to be good. I said I would.

It was the hot part of the afternoon when we set out. Sylvie was taking a nap and so was Geronimo, but we pulled him out from under the porch and made him come along.

When I say the hot part of the afternoon I mean *hot!* There wasn't even a breeze. Nothing. We were too hot even to play at being in a South American jungle with pythons draped from the trees. We just walked Indian file slapping at gnats, scratching at chigger bites, and sweating.

We passed the swimming hole and it looked *good*, let me tell you, but we resisted the temptation.

When we got to the wire fence, stretched across the creek, that separated us from the army land, there was a big official-looking red sign between the strands of wire. *No Trespassing. Violators Will Be Prosecuted.* But we just crawled under the wire, getting our knees wet, and kept on going.

The funny thing was that it felt different on that side of the fence. It made me feel that maybe every time I put my foot down something might blow up in my face.

"Do the soldiers ever come into this part?" I asked.

"Hardly ever."

Before we'd gone very far, Lonnie made us get out of the creek so he could find the pear trees again. He thought if he could find them he'd be able to see just where it was he'd seen Butchie and Leroy come out of the woods with the dead rabbit that other time.

Once we left the water it was worse than ever. The weeds were all grown up and there were lots of little trees and brambles and vines. We just had to trust to luck because we couldn't even see half the time where we were putting our feet down. Geronimo got excited about a smell and went off on a crazy zigzag through the bushes, just his tail showing and waving back and forth. We hoped the noise he was making would scare away any snakes.

After we got through the woods we came to a big open space where there were just weeds and cedar trees and it was easier going. Lonnie thought the pear trees were on the hill just in front of us, so we climbed up there, and, sure enough, there they were with the little green pears growing on them.

Lonnie got his bearings from that spot, and we ran down the hill again and came to the creek at the place that Lonnie thought was right.

"OK," I said as we walked along the edge of the creek, "now how do we find the traps?"

That was a problem, since the whole thing about a trap is that it's hidden. Lonnie said we should get long sticks and poke at the brush and stuff all along the edges of the creek, so we did that.

"If you step in a trap it might break your ankle," Lonnie added, so I was careful about where I stepped and poked.

We went up and down the creek for quite a distance without finding anything and I was starting to get pretty discouraged. It was all so grown up, and there were so many clumps that could have hidden a trap, that I couldn't see that we had any chance.

"It's a good idea, Lonnie," I said, "but I don't think it's going to work."

"I dunno," Lonnie said. We stood still for a minute, taking a rest and watching Geronimo, who was wading through the water and heading up the bank. He had a perfect nose for anything that smelled like food, and he'd evidently found something because he started eating on the bank.

"I bet it's a stinking old fish," Lonnie said. "Hey, Geronimo!"

Geronimo always ignored his name if it didn't suit him to come, so he went on eating whatever it was. By the time we got there he'd nearly polished it off. We saw him eat the last bite.

"Hey, wait a minute!" Lonnie told him, but Geronimo just wiped his tongue around his mouth. "Didn't that look like dog food?" Lonnie asked me.

It clicked in both our heads at the same minute. Dog food doesn't get onto a creek bank by magic, and if somebody put it there they must have had a reason.

"Bait for a trap!" we said together. Lonnie grabbed Geronimo's collar and I poked with my stick in the bushes right behind the spot where the dog food had been, and sure enough, we heard the snap as the trap shut on the tip of my stick. We pulled aside the bushes and there it was: a black trap with teeth like a shark, the whole thing fastened down to a tree root. It was mean looking and I didn't like to think what would happen to any animal that put its foot in it. I snapped off my stick and threw away the broken piece. When I did that, I saw something else that was going to be a big help. On a tree two feet away, there was a little white nick cut in the bark.

"They mark them!" I said excitedly. "That's so they can find the places themselves without any trouble."

It was as easy as figuring out a message written in a code you understood. All we had to do was walk down the bank looking for white nicks on the trees, and whenever we saw one we'd grab Geronimo's collar until we had poked around enough to spring the trap, and then we'd let Geronimo eat the bait. We found six traps altogether and they were all empty.

It tickled us to think about Leroy and Butchie finding all their traps sprung and the bait gone. Geronimo had gotten a free supper for himself off the deal, too.

We'd come a long way upstream by now and we didn't want to go back the way we'd come, so we cut through the woods until we came to an open place. About twenty yards ahead of us there was a military road. "Let's risk it," I said. "It'll be a lot easier walking on the road, and if we head west we're bound to come to the highway sooner or later."

"OK by me," Lonnie said.

So we were just walking along, laughing and not keeping an eye out the way we should have been, when somebody yelled at us, "You kids! Come here!"

Up on a little rise and sitting under a big tree there were two soldiers. We were caught for sure, and there was nothing for it but to walk over to them. One was sprawled on the ground with his hands under his head and the other was sitting, leaning against the tree.

"What're you kids doing here?" the one leaning against the tree said.

"My dog got lost in here and we were just finding him," Lonnie said very fast. Geronimo came plodding up just then with his tongue hanging down about a foot. If he'd ever been lost in his life he didn't look like it.

"Got lost, huh?" the soldier said, nudging the other one with his elbow. "We were wondering where we were ourselves. You wouldn't know how far the highway is from here, would you?"

"Nope," Lonnie said. "We were heading that way ourselves."

"All in the same boat, huh? I'm Wesley and that's Art trying to sleep under the tree." We told them our names and sat down in the thin little shade with them. Wesley might have been my dad's age, but Art didn't look much older than a high-school kid.

"You all have your guns with you?" Lonnie asked, although it was pretty clear that if those two soldiers had guns they must be sitting on them.

"We're ambulance corps," Art said from under the cap he'd put over his face for shade. "Got separated from the rest of our outfit and decided we might as well cool off. We're not all that anxious to die of a heatstroke. Man! This heat."

"Shoot," Lonnie said. "We've been out here all afternoon and hadn't hardly noticed it, have we, Ben?"

"No," I said. But that was a bald-faced lie.

"We're from Maine," Wesley said, "so the heat just about kills us."

"I'm from New York and it doesn't bother _me_," I bragged. "My grandmother lives here, and I come every summer."

"Oh, yeah? I've got a little boy at home just about like you two. Name's Fred."

Wesley opened up his wallet and showed us a photograph. It was a school picture with a blue-sky kind of background and this kid grinning, showing his teeth.

There didn't seem to be much to say about it, so we just nodded our heads. Art rolled over so he could see too, and when he did that I saw something that made my heart practically stop beating. He'd been using a comic book as a headrest and one glimpse was all I needed.

"That's a Daredevil number one!" I shouted, pointing at it.

The others just looked at me like I was crazy. "Daredevil number one!" I said again. "The first issue of Daredevil published. Where'd it come from?"

I picked it up carefully and smoothed it out. There was a dented place where the soldier had been lying on it and it was a little worn around the edges, but not bad.

"Lying around the barracks," Art said. "The magazines lying around there go back practically to year one. I just stuck it in my pack this morning thinking I might want something to read."

"Listen," I said, my voice going tight, "could I have this? I collect comics, and I'd really like to have this one."

"Sure, take it," Art said. "Nobody's going to miss it."

"Oh, boy," I said. "Thanks."

Wesley gave us two pieces of Juicy Fruit gum, and we were just settling down to enjoy ourselves, when we saw a big cloud of dust coming down the road. Wesley took one look and said, "Uh oh, kids. Looks like our company's about to catch up with us. You'd better scoot off before they see you."

We didn't have any choice. We had to say good-bye and run back down the slope to the woods and the creek. We were doomed to going home that way whether we wanted to or not.

It was late afternoon by this time, and the shadows were getting long, and I began to feel a little uneasy. I tried to take my mind off the gnats and mosquitoes and that uneasy feeling by thinking what fun it was going to be to write Richard and tell him I had Daredevil number one. And for free. He'd die. He really would. How I wished I could run across the road and show it to him the way I would if I were at home. But, then, if I were at home Art wouldn't have given me Daredevil number one, either, so you can't win.

When we got to the fence and crawled under the *No Trespassing* sign something really felt wrong. I looked hard at the creek banks and the water but there didn't seem to be anything out of the way. Since it was late afternoon the birds were stirring around a lot in the trees and I could hear two doves and a mockingbird singing. But that was all.

It was lucky that we were walking along without talking, because we heard the voices when they were still a way off.

"Leroy and Butchie!" Lonnie whispered.

We ran out of the water and scrambled up the bank looking for a place to hide. There was a big tree with bushes growing around it not far from the bank, and we ducked behind it. I stuck Daredevil number one under my belt and pulled my shirt over it. We'd just gotten settled when Leroy and Butchie came sauntering along the bank laughing and talking.

At the same moment we saw something else. That dumb Geronimo was still wading around in the water as unconcerned as a newt.

"Hey, that's the dog that belongs to those two kids," Butchie said when he saw him. "If he's here, they must be around here someplace too. You go that way and I'll go this, Leroy."

The Mannings started beating the bushes up and down the creek bank and Geronimo just stood there in the creek grinning. I kept telling him under my breath to stay where he was and not to come looking for us. But it wasn't Geronimo who gave us away. It was that crazy Lonnie.

"Let's give 'em a run for their money," Lonnie said, nudging me in the ribs, and I was so taken by surprise I just looked back at him with my mouth open. Before I could even grab him he was standing up and yelling, "We're up here, you big dumb oxes!" and he was off and running like a rabbit. I didn't have any choice but to run too.

"You stupid!" I yelled at his back. "Why didn't you keep your mouth shut?"

He just laughed. It was easy for him. He was a good runner; he could really zigzag around those trees and bushes. We were climbing the slope up from the creek and I was having a hard time keeping up. Lonnie was pretty far ahead of me. And then, at the top of the slope, he just disappeared. I didn't even know which direction he'd gone in. Oh, swell, Lonnie, I thought. You get us in this fix, and then you disappear.

I couldn't take time to be mad at Lonnie right then, though, because one of the Mannings was crashing along behind me like a bear. I tried to run faster, keeping in mind that the creek was over my right shoulder. As I was worrying about whoever was following me, Butchie jumped out from behind a bush in front of me, his arms wide as a net. I let out a squeal and ran to my left. I thought Leroy was still behind me somewhere, but maybe I started running in the wrong direction by mistake, because all of a sudden he was just there, right in front of me, and all he had to do was reach out those long skinny arms of his and catch me.

"Hey, I got 'im," Leroy called out to Butchie, and he came running up, grinning like a dog.

"Wonder what he's got on 'im," Leroy said, picking me up and flipping me over so he was holding me by my ankles.

Of course when he did that my shirt fell in front of my face and Daredevil number one slid out of my belt and fell to the ground. I could see it just under my head.

"Look at that," Butchie said, picking it up.

"That's mine!" I yelled, feeling an awful sinking feeling. It was terrible to have your hands on a Daredevil number one and then lose it again just like that.

"Possession is nine-tenths of the law," Butchie said. "What else you got?"

I didn't have anything.

"Put me down," I said, my voice sounding funny because the blood had rushed to my head.

"Do what he says, Leroy, put him down," Butchie said, so of course Leroy just dropped me in a heap. It's a wonder my neck wasn't broken.

"You could kill a person like that," I said, sitting up and rubbing my head.

"Do tell," Butchie said. "We could've broke his delicate little neck, Leroy." I saw my Daredevil rolled up and stuck in his back pocket, but there wasn't anything I could do. How I wished I could become the Tarantula all of a sudden and shoot out tranquilizing darts from my hands.

"Where do you come from, anyway, kid?" Butchie said.

"New York."

"Ho, boy!" Butchie said, slapping his hand on his thigh. "Is it right what I hear about everybody in New York going around barefooted?"

"Sure," I said, trying to bluff it out that way.

"You hear that?" Butchie said, sounding like I'd given him the best answer he could have dreamed up. "He says he don't need his shoes, Leroy."

"Well, if he don't need 'em we might's well take 'em," Leroy said, and he'd grabbed my sneakers off my feet and my socks too before I could say anything. He stuck the socks in his pockets, but he and Butchie used my shoes to throw back and forth as they ran off, heading up the creek.

When they were out of sight, I got up and started heading down to the creek. The rocks were sharp, there were prickly pears to watch out for, and my feet weren't very tough. I knew Mom was going to be really mad when I got home without my shoes. All I had left now were my Sunday ones. But the thing that made me feel worse was losing Daredevil number one. That just wasn't fair!

I was really mad at Lonnie when I found him where I knew he would be, under Jesse's bridge. It didn't help when he started laughing at me, either.

"You better keep your mouth shut, Lonnie, I'm mad at you." I went straight through the camp and up to the highway; Jesse wasn't there anyway.

"You just look funny walking like that."

"You'd look funny too if they took your shoes. They took my Daredevil, too. It's all your fault, Lonnie."

"I thought you were right behind me, Ben, honest."

"You didn't have to yell at them in the first place."

Even though I walked in the grass along the side

of the highway the rocks still hurt my feet, but I was too mad at Lonnie to take much notice.

We walked along for quite a while without saying anything.

"You could wear my shoes, Ben," Lonnie said after a long spell. "I'm used to going barefooted."

At first I ignored him, but then my feet really hurt and I didn't think I was going to get home that way. "OK," I said.

Lonnie gave me his shoes right away and I knew he felt bad about what had happened. I didn't feel quite as mad at him after I got his shoes on. They pinched, but that was better than being barefooted.

When we got to his turning I told him I'd meet him at five o'clock the next morning to spring the traps before Leroy and Butchie would get there, and I gave him his shoes back.

All Mom said when I got home was that if I lost any more shoes they'd have to come out of my allowance.

Grandma said, "You right sure that little Lester boy isn't leading you into trouble?" And of course I had to say no, he certainly wasn't. But I don't know. Somehow wherever Lonnie was, there was trouble lying in wait.

# Chapter

## 4

That night there was a humdinger of a storm, and I think the cloud must've come to rest for a while right above Grandma's house. A great purple light would flash, and before I could even start counting, the thunder would practically bounce me out of bed. I thought I could even smell the lightning — a kind of dry, sizzling smell.

After a while there was a space between the lightning and the thunder, and then the rain started coming down in sheets. I could hear Grandma and Mom running around the house shutting windows. I got up and shut my own, but even so, some wind must've gotten in because Uncle Warren's airplanes danced around in the lightning flashes like they were about to take off and go.

I love the sound of rain on the roof. It's one of my favorite sounds. I just lay there listening to it and

planning to stay awake until five when I was supposed to meet Lonnie. But I couldn't do it. That
sound of rain is a sleepy sound and I went to sleep
without even knowing it.

I didn't open my eyes again until the light was
coming in, bright, and the birds were singing like
crazy. I grabbed my watch from under my pillow and
held it up. Five-twenty! I got my clothes on in two
minutes and went as softly as I could through the
house to the front door.

I shut the door very softly behind me and ran.
I was so busy running, just listening to the sound of
my shoes against the road, that I was halfway to
Lonnie's before I noticed what a beautiful morning
it was. The air was clear and fresh, not a bit hot, and
there were puddles in the road and along the ditches.
Birds hopped in and out of the puddles taking baths,
and I thought it was worth getting up that early to
see everything so untouched.

Of course Lonnie was waiting for me. I didn't
even stop when I came up to him. "Come on, Lonnie,"
I called out. "I know it's my fault we're late but I've
got to be back in an hour."

"I don't know if we can," he said, falling in beside
me.

"Well, Grandma gets up at six-thirty and I better
be at least in the yard by then."

But luck was with us. Since it was cooler we
could run faster, and we didn't have any trouble

finding the traps because the trees were wet and dark and the notches cut in them showed up very white. The food Leroy and Butchie had put out for bait had all washed away, which disappointed Geronimo, but we were relieved because no animals had come out in the night to be caught in the traps. The only thing we had to remember was to rub away the tracks our shoes made on the wet ground.

By six-twenty-five we were coming up the road to the house. Geronimo disappeared into one of the fields after a rabbit, and Lonnie and I just ambled along, thinking about breakfast.

"Why don't you eat breakfast with me?" I asked, and Lonnie was saying maybe or something like that when we both saw the same thing at the same moment. A bird standing by the side of the road.

Bigger than a robin, he was a reddish brown bird who was turning his head from side to side. I thought he'd fly away when we got up close but he didn't, and Lonnie reached down and picked him up just like you'd pick up a cat.

"Screech owl," Lonnie said. "See his ear tufts?"

"*I* know that," I said. Lonnie always thinks he knows everything.

When Lonnie held him up we could see the reason he wasn't trying to get away. One of his eyes was round and golden but the other was shut and the feathers looked damp around it.

"He must've flown into a tree last night in the

storm," Lonnie said. "Or maybe into the side of a car."

The owl closed his talons around Lonnie's finger and rode like that, fluttering his wings a little so he could keep his balance.

"Doesn't he hurt your finger, sticking his claws in like that?" I asked.

"Nope," Lonnie said. "Just pinches some. He can sure hang on."

The owl didn't seem afraid and he didn't seem to mind at all when we ran our fingers over his feathers. I'd never seen an owl up close before and I couldn't get over how soft his feathers were. There were layers and layers of them and they were a lot thicker and softer somehow than a chicken's feathers.

"Isn't that the softest thing you ever felt?" I said to Lonnie.

"That's so he can fly and not make any noise," Lonnie said, showing off again.

"Let's take him in the house and see if he wants anything to eat," I said.

The owl watched us as we carried him to the house. He'd turn his head one way and then the other to keep us both in view, and it was funny because he could turn his head around so he was looking directly behind him. It looked like he was trying to unscrew his head.

Grandma was already in the kitchen in her bathrobe, filling up the coffeepot.

"My, my," she said when we brought the owl in. "A little screech owl. Well, I declare. Just sitting there as pretty as a picture."

"We found him in the road," I told her. "One of his eyes is hurt. Do you have any meat we could give him?"

Grandma was measuring coffee into the pot, and she doesn't like being interrupted when she's in the middle of a job. "Just hold your horses," she said. "Can't you see I've got my hands full? And don't you hold him over the table. Mind out, now. Hold him over there by the door."

So we had to stand on the mat that said COME IN and pat the owl so he wouldn't get nervous. After Grandma got the coffeepot plugged in she took a beef roast out of the refrigerator and cut off some little pieces.

I put a piece of meat on my finger and held it out to the owl. It made me uneasy because that owl's beak was meant for use. If he could tear up a mouse with it he could do the same thing to my finger.

He saw the meat all right and started eyeing it, bending his head down to get a good look. And then he stretched out his neck and took it off my finger as neatly as you please. He didn't touch my finger with his beak at all. I had the feeling that he knew my finger wasn't for eating.

Every time we gave him a piece of meat he

swallowed it and watched us to see if we were going to give him more.

"He sure is tame," I said. "Maybe he was somebody's pet owl who got away."

"Naw. It's just because he's hurt," Lonnie said.

Grandma said Lonnie couldn't stand there all morning with an owl on his finger, so she went off to find the cage she'd had for parakeets until they'd died.

Mom came into the kitchen in time to help us slide open the bottom of the cage to put the owl inside. He didn't want to turn loose of Lonnie's finger but he finally did, and we managed to slide the bottom of the cage shut.

It wasn't a big enough cage for a bird as big as an owl. He couldn't even spread out his wings in it and he couldn't move more than three or four steps forward and back. I could see that we couldn't keep him long in a little cage like that.

"I wonder if he's going to be blind in one eye," Mom said.

I said I thought maybe we should take him to a vet but neither Mom nor Grandma thought a vet would know much about owls.

"I bet I know somebody who would," Lonnie said. "You know that lady who's bought the old Harriman place up by the river? She's the one always going around with field glasses looking at birds. I bet she'd know, if anybody did."

"I declare," Grandma said. "I think you're right.

It's that Mrs. Tanksley he's talking about," she said to Mom. "Moved here last year. A queer one. Some folks around here take to her, and some don't. But if it's one thing she knows it's probably birds. I'll telephone her directly after breakfast."

While Grandma made biscuits and Mom set the table, Lonnie and I took the owl in his cage to the living room where we'd be out of the way.

I set him down on the little table by the window and we looked through the bars at him, where the light made all kinds of colors show up in his feathers.

"He'd like it over at my house," Lonnie said. "I could hang the cage in a tree right outside the back door and he'd feel at home up there in the leaves."

I didn't like that idea at all. I'd never had any thought but that we'd keep the owl at my house.

"He'd be safer here," I said. "Sylvie might let him out at your house or the rattlesnake might come back and get him."

"Rattlesnakes can't swallow full-grown owls," Lonnie said. "Don't you know anything? Anyhow, I was the one saw him first."

"You were not. We saw him the same time."

"I was the one picked him up. You wouldn't have picked him up in a month of Sundays. You're scared to pick him up right now."

"I am not! I fed him and I wasn't scared."

"You don't know anything about owls, and that's not all you don't know, either."

"Listen here, Lonnie. You got us into that mess yesterday and I lost my shoes and Daredevil number one, so you better not say another word. The cage is mine; how are you going to keep an owl without a cage?"

"I'll find something. It's too little for him anyway."

We were practically shouting at each other when Mom called us in to eat breakfast. Lonnie picked up the cage but I grabbed hold of it too and wouldn't let go. When Mom called again, sounding mad, we set the cage down carefully, watching each other while we did, and went in to the kitchen. I knew Lonnie didn't want to sit down at the table, but he didn't want to leave me with the owl, either, so he had to sit with me.

Although we were sitting side by side, we kept our heads turned away from each other. Mom and Grandma were too busy talking to notice anything, and Lonnie and I just sat there eating biscuits and not saying a word. Every time I pushed the jar of strawberry preserves over in Lonnie's direction he pushed it back. He ate his biscuits plain without even any butter, probably because he was too proud to ask for it.

"At home I drink coffee," Lonnie finally said, not even cutting an eye in my direction.

"Aw, you don't."

"Do too. I like it with milk and sugar."

"Tastes bitter."

"Not when you get used to it."

"Bet that's why you're so stunted. Drinking coffee."

He gave me a furious look. "Name one thing you can do I can't."

"Swim something besides the dog paddle."

"I stay up!"

"Not for long, you couldn't."

"As long as you could, I bet."

We sat there stiffer than ever, pretending the other wasn't anywhere about. But it's hard to keep that up for long. It gets to be boring after a while. So I finally said, "Listen, Lonnie, maybe we could take turns with the owl. You could take him for a night and I could keep him for a night."

Lonnie just shrugged his shoulders, but he didn't say no.

When we finished eating we went back into the living room to see how the owl was doing. His feathers were hunched up around his shoulders and he didn't look too happy.

We were poking our fingers in the cage trying to cheer him up when Grandma came to the door to say that she'd telephoned the woman who knew a lot about birds, and she said she'd be glad to take a look at our owl.

Mom called from the kitchen that after she helped Grandma with the dishes she'd drive us over.

But when I found out from Lonnie that it was only a mile and a half I said that it was OK, we'd walk.

Lonnie jabbed me with his elbow, but I shook my head for him to keep quiet. "It's a nice morning after the rain and it'll be fun to walk," I called to Mom.

"What'd you do that for?" Lonnie said when we'd started down the road heading north, the owl cage between us.

"If she'd come along she'd have talked to the bird woman all the time herself, and we wouldn't have gotten a word in edgeways. You know how grown-ups are. And he is our owl."

But it wasn't long before we both wished we'd let Mom drive us. We had to take turns carrying the cage by the metal loop in the top. That loop really dug into our fingers, and the cage got so heavy that by the time we got to the bird-woman's driveway, our fingers were so worn out we kept trading the cage back and forth about every three minutes.

The bird-woman's house was near the river, on a hill, and there were woods all around it so you couldn't see the house from the road. But you knew the minute you came to her land, because there was a good, strong barbed-wire fence all around it with lots of *No Hunting, No Trespassing* signs hanging on the fence and nailed up on trees. Most of the signs had rusty holes where somebody had shot them.

When we got to the driveway there was a gate

across that was locked shut, so we had to climb over. I was glad that Grandma had telephoned because if the bird woman hadn't been expecting us, I don't think I would have had the courage to go up the driveway. It was a long drive with woods on both sides, and the house still not in sight.

We were poking along, going slower and slower, when suddenly someone called out, "Helloooo!" It was strange because the noise came from somewhere up in the air. We were turning around and around in the driveway, looking up at the sky, when the voice said, "Over here!" So we started through the woods on the left side of the road, stumbling along since we kept looking up.

Then we came out in this little clearing, and there was a kind of tower — a platform on the top of four long poles with a ladder going up to it. There was a woman up there looking down at us. She was wearing one of those hats that African explorers wear in movies. I'd never seen a real hat like that before.

"Stop staring and come on up, boys," she said. "There's the ladder."

I could tell she was one of those kind of people who are used to having other people do what they say. My fourth-grade teacher was like that. Miss Peabody. She had red hair that always looked like she slept on it wrong and she wore this ratty-looking sweater with sagging pockets. But when she said jump, you said how high.

"I don't think I can get up there with the owl," I said.

The bird woman peered down at me as though she wondered if I had good sense. "Why, set him down, then. He'll be all right down there."

So I set the cage on the ground and climbed up behind Lonnie.

The bird woman was sitting on a folding canvas stool with a pair of binoculars hanging around her neck and a notebook in her lap. She was wearing a pair of leather boots that came to her knees, and her jeans were stuck in them. She had to be nearly as old as Grandma because all of her hair that you could see sticking out from under the explorer's hat was grey, but I absolutely couldn't imagine Grandma wearing boots like that and jeans.

I guess she saw I was staring at her, because she said, "Well, what do you think of the crazy bird woman?"

I felt myself going hot, and although I opened my mouth, no words would come out.

She only laughed. "Don't be bothered by what I say. Too used to living by myself with nothing but birds to talk to. I can guess what a strange duck the people around here think I am. And maybe I am odd, but I'm too old to care. My name's Myra."

"I'm Ben," I said and turned to look around at Lonnie, but Lonnie was just kicking his toe against the platform. It was the first time I'd seen Lonnie turn shy over anything, but I could see that the cat had really gotten his tongue this time, as Grandma would say. So I added, "And this is Lonnie," since it didn't look like he would say anything.

"Hear that?" Myra said, raising one finger to show that we should be quiet. I could hear lots of birds singing, but I didn't know what I was supposed to be listening for.

"That sweet little curl of birdsong. Hear it? There!"

I looked over at Lonnie for help and saw he still had that silly look on his face.

"I didn't think you'd know. That's a bluebird. Remember it now. How many bluebirds have you heard in your life? I have four pairs in nesting boxes."

I could see that she could go on all day talking about birds, but right then I was too worried about our owl to listen.

"About our owl — one of his eyes is hurt," I said, "and we're scared he might be blind."

"Oh, yes," Myra said. "Your owl. Well, let's go have a look."

We helped her gather up her things and we all climbed down the ladder.

Myra looked at our owl in the cage, and he looked back at her with his one yellow eye.

"Well, well," she said. "I've got some antibiotic salve we'll try for his eye. And that cage is too small

for him. Look at the poor thing. He can hardly turn
around in there."

She picked up the cage and headed for the house
in a lope. Lonnie and I had to trot to keep up.

We passed through an enclosed porch where
there were a lot of plants, through the kitchen, and
into the living room where Myra finally set the cage
down on the floor and opened up a big wicker chest.
She'd taken out two armloads of blankets from the
chest and stuck newspapers in the bottom before
Lonnie and I could say a word. When she went off to
find the antibiotic salve I said quickly to Lonnie,
"She's awfully bossy. She's going to take over everything if we don't watch it. We better name that owl
in a hurry so at least she'll remember it's ours. You
got any ideas?"

Lonnie just shook his head. He was too busy
staring around the room to be any use. I wanted to
stare, too, but I didn't take time except for a quick
look around. There were so many things to see we
could have spent half a day looking at all of it. The
walls were covered with all kinds of stuff, wooden
masks and giant kites with eyes painted on them.
Right beside where we were standing there was a
brass elephant holding up a coffee table. Everywhere
I looked there was something different. But I tried to
keep my mind on our owl and the problem I could
see we were going to have with Myra.

"Would you care if we named him Wol?" I asked Lonnie. "That's the name that's been in the back of my mind. You know, in *Winnie-the-Pooh* there was this owl who could write but not spell, so he always wrote his name Wol."

Lonnie didn't say yes or no, so I said, "I guess that's all right then," just as Myra came back.

She didn't need any help getting Wol out of the parakeet cage, and she had the salve in his eye and had put him in the chest and shut the lid before a person could have sneezed.

"His name is Wol," I said very quickly and firmly. "You can keep him for a while in that chest, but we'll come back in the morning to give him his breakfast. He's already eaten this morning."

"Don't make it too late, then," Myra said. "I'm not one of those people who sit around rocking in the shade."

Lonnie, who hadn't said a word up to now, suddenly pointed to something hanging on the wall. "What's that thing?" he said.

I turned my head and looked at this crazy mask hanging on the wall. One eye was higher than the other one and its mouth had this terrible expression as though it had just bitten down on something that tasted terrible.

"Oh, that's from New Zealand," Myra said. "My husband, Tremain, and I traveled all over the world, or over most of it anyhow, at one time or another, and we picked up things wherever we went. Tremain was an engineer, an engineer of bridges, that is, and we went all over the world building bridges. India, Japan, Liberia. You name it and we've probably been there building a bridge over some muddy river or another. Here, have a look at these. I know what boys are like, wanting to get their fingers on everything."

She picked up two drums and put them in front of me. One was tall and skinny and one was shorter and fatter. They kind of reminded me of Leroy and Butchie, to tell the truth. "Talking drums from Ghana," she said. "Go on. See what they sound like."

"What do they say?" I said, looking at them doubtfully. I had the idea that if I hit one it would say "Ouch" or something like that.

Myra didn't answer. She was too busy handing a curved knife in a scabbard to Lonnie. It was curved like a new moon and sharp-enough looking to cut somebody in two. He started inching it out of the holder very carefully and I knew he was as uneasy with it as I was with the talking drums. I gave them two little taps with my fingers, but they just sounded like any other drums to me. If that was talking, it wasn't English.

Myra picked up a little pot from the mantelpiece and held it up. An ordinary-looking little fat, white pot. "Guess what's in here?" she said.

Well, naturally we couldn't.

"Tremain," she said. I heard Lonnie drawing in his breath.

"His ashes actually. He always said when he died he wanted to be cremated, so when he had his heart attack and died in Bombay, I did what he wanted. But I couldn't see any point in leaving him there, and when I came home I couldn't see any point in leaving him anywhere else either, so I just keep his ashes with me. Some people may find that terrible but it seems perfectly natural to me."

I imagined Tremain inside the little white pot like the genie in Aladdin's lamp. I didn't want to rub it, that's for sure.

"There's a squirrel climbing up your table leg," Lonnie pointed out.

"That's Bertram," Myra said. "I keep his nuts in a bowl on the table and that's why he's climbing the leg. You shouldn't try to pick up Bertram, because he bites."

Bertram fingered over the nuts in the bowl and finally took out a small, skinny pecan and started gnawing it, making a rasping noise.

"Oh, I must give Willie a whistle," Myra said. "You'll love Willie."

She gave a good, sharp whistle and immediately the living-room door started to rattle. "Who's Willie, anyway?" Lonnie said, looking alarmed. I knew what he was thinking because I was thinking the same thing myself. What if Willie were a ghost or something like that? I didn't care at all for the way that door handle was turning by itself.

But when the door swung open an animal jumped out on the floor, and I saw we didn't have to worry. Willie was a raccoon. He came wobbling across the room toward us and climbed into Myra's lap like a cat and rolled on his back to have his stomach patted.

"He loves raisins," Myra said. "Get that jar from the high bookshelf."

So I did, and Willie took raisins out of our hands with his paws and put them in his mouth very neatly without spilling many.

Suddenly a loud noise came from the yard, which made Willie bolt from Myra's lap and Bertram disappear from the table. Myra leaped up yelling, "Hellions!" and ran out the door, so Lonnie and I ran out too.

"What was that noise?" I asked Lonnie as we came through the back door.

"Shotgun, sounded to me like."

Myra was running around the yard like a bird dog on a trail and we ran around too but I didn't even know what I was supposed to be looking for. Then Myra was off like a shot for a bird feeder under a clump of trees. When we got there she was down on the ground picking up two dead birds that were lying in the grass. I knew they were dead all right because their heads wobbled back against her fingers.

"A dove and a nuthatch, and why, may I ask you?" Myra said sadly, holding out her hands. "Spite! Pure spite, that's what. Oh, I wish I could get my hands on those two!"

"What two is that?" I asked, although I thought I already knew.

"Two boys I ran off my land last fall when they were quail hunting. Not only once, let me tell you, but three times. The last time I threatened them with the sheriff and I would have been all too happy to carry through. Since then they've done nothing but harass me. Cutting my fence, shooting up my signs, letting their dog run wild through my land. And this isn't the first time they've shot my birds."

"What kind of a dog have they got?" Lonnie asked.

"A mutt. I don't know what mix. A big ugly thing with little spots all over him is all I know."

"Sounds to me like a blue tick hound," Lonnie said. He looked at me, and I looked at him, and of course I knew what he was thinking. It had to be Leroy and Butchie with their mean dog. Should we tell or not? I shook my head *no*. I could look ahead and see how it would be if we told all we knew. Myra would take over the whole thing and it wouldn't be ours anymore, the way she'd taken over Wol. No, I'd rather we handled it on our own. We were doing OK by ourselves.

We helped Myra bury the birds, and then she

insisted we stay and have some cookies to eat, and what with one thing and another the whole morning went like that.

I was late getting back to Grandma's for lunch, and then I wasn't hungry because of the cookies, so Grandma and Mom were cross. Also I missed Wol because it isn't every day you find a tame owl and somebody else takes him over, so, I don't know, things just weren't very good. I had the bad feeling, too, that they were probably going to get worse.

Which they did.

# Chapter

## 5

Late the very next afternoon when we went to spring the traps, there was this bad surprise waiting for us. We were in a hurry and we'd sprung three of the traps in nothing flat, but when we came to the fourth there was a piece of paper on the ground, held down at the corners by rocks.

YOU BETTER STOP. WE'LL GET YOU IF YOU DON'T.

"They know," Lonnie said when we read that.

"What do they know?" I said, being very smart about the whole thing. "They can't know it's us because if they already knew it was us they wouldn't fool around with leaving a note. All they know is that something fishy's going on."

74

Well, of course they had figured that out. Traps don't get sprung without catching anything unless somebody's springing them. You don't have to be a genius to know that.

"Let's just spring the rest of those traps and get out of here," I said, leaping up.

We were lucky because the Mannings hadn't waited around. Maybe they thought their warning would scare anybody away.

We were relieved, of course, not to see them, but I knew that wouldn't be the end of it. Now they knew somebody was springing their traps, they wouldn't let it rest. So on the way home I asked Lonnie to spend the night with me so we could make plans.

He said he guessed that would be OK and our mothers said it would be all right, so Lonnie came over to my house just at dinner time with his things in a paper sack. We sat down at the table to eat nearly as soon as he came in so I didn't have a chance to say anything to him.

As soon as he slid into his seat, he picked up his piece of cornbread and took a bite out of it before I could nudge him. I knew Grandma was going to close her eyes and say grace, which she did, and Lonnie had to stop chewing until she'd stopped. He was like a person playing statues and caught in a bad position.

That got him all embarrassed, and after that he didn't say anything and didn't eat much, although Mom and Grandma kept trying to get him to.

"You'll shrivel up and blow away in a big wind if you don't eat any more than that," Grandma said, but he still just picked at his food.

Actually, I knew just how he felt. I don't like eating at my friends' houses either. It's a strange thing, but even very ordinary food like macaroni and cheese tastes different when Richard's mother cooks it. There's something funny about it I don't like. And I'm always afraid I'm going to be faced with something terrible to eat, like one time at my friend Kenneth's house they were having spinach pie and his mother was one of those kind that practically forces the food down your throat. There's just one thing that spinach pie makes me think of and it's not a thing you can mention while other people are trying to eat. However, I was hit with inspiration and said that I thought I was allergic to spinach and had better just stick to bread. I could tell Kenneth's mother didn't believe me, but there wasn't anything she could do about it. The only thing I trust to eat in other people's houses is pizza bought at Pizza Kitchen or somewhere. It tastes the same wherever you eat it. So I knew how Lonnie felt, although I couldn't pass that information on to him. I got us excused from the table as soon as I could, and we went outside where Lonnie revived. We went down to the tree house to play while it was still daylight. I found poor old Bernie there where I'd left him since that first day when Lonnie climbed up to the tree house, and I took him home when we left at dusk. The whippoorwills in the woods were calling that sort of sad noise they make, and the fireflies were lighting up all across the pasture.

"Ned and I used to catch fireflies and put them in a jar until we'd get so many it would be lighted up like a lantern," I said. I really missed Ned all of a sudden. It used to be fun running around the front yard catching fireflies while Grandma and Mom and Dad sat on the porch and talked.

The dew had fallen, and our feet were wet by the time we got to the house, but by then it was time to go to bed anyway.

Lonnie hadn't brought along any pajamas so I didn't wear mine either, even though I don't really like sleeping in my underwear. I wanted him to feel at home. "Hey, Lonnie," I said. "Want to read a comic?"

He shrugged his shoulders but I tossed him over a Daredevil anyway. I knew he couldn't resist it and I was right. Pretty soon he was really making those pages turn. So I read some myself and kept quiet so he could finish it before I turned out the light.

"We've got business to discuss," I said.

Somehow, it was hard to think in the dark with the moonlight coming in the windows and making weird white bars across the floor, so I got out my flashlight and flashed it around the room. It gave everything a better feeling.

"I been thinking, Lonnie," I said, watching my

flashlight make big circles around the ceiling. "Maybe we ought to just forget about those traps. If we keep springing them we're going to get caught sooner or later."

"No, sir," Lonnie said. "You can stop if you want to, but I'm going ahead. I don't think the Tarantula and the Red Chigger should give up over a little thing like that."

Well, of course, since he put it that way I could see that we couldn't back down.

"I hate to think what's going to happen to us if they catch us. That's all."

"We won't let 'em catch us."

"They just *did* catch me."

"We'll have to fight 'em off. I can whip any of the sixth-grade boys now and I bet I could take on a seventh grader."

"The Mannings are older than that, Lonnie," I said. But I could also see that there wasn't any way out of it. "OK, then. The Tarantula and the Red Chigger forever. Right?"

"Right," Lonnie said.

We shook hands on it, reaching across in the dark.

"You ever get scared at night?" I asked Lonnie then, now that the other was settled.

"Nope. You?"

"No."

That was a bald-faced lie. At home sometimes I wake up in the middle of the night and I'm just sure I hear somebody walking real softly up the walk to our door. I can hear it as plain as anything — that noise sneakers make on concrete. And then I hear the front door open very, very quietly and footsteps coming up the stairs. They don't ever come in my door, though. Just up the stairs. And to tell the truth, even when I'm sure I hear the footsteps, I know I'm making them up. Ned says I hear footsteps because I read too many comics and watch too much television, but I don't think that's it. I'll bet that boys living in log cabins in the frontier days used to hear bears or Indians creeping up through the woods when there wasn't anything there.

"My daddy knows some pretty scary stories," Lonnie said. "Haints and casting charms and stuff like that. They could pretty nearly make you scared."

"Well, I'll put my flashlight on the floor between the beds," I said. "If either one of us needs it, it'll be right there."

I went off to sleep quickly the way I always do, but I woke up suddenly in the middle of the night. I could hear somebody moving around on the other side of the room.

"What is it?" I said, sitting straight up and throwing the sheet back. I forgot all about Lonnie until he spoke up.

"I figure I better go home," he said.

"It's still *dark* outside. You don't want to go home now."

He already had his shirt on and was reaching for his pants.

"No, I think I better go. I look after Sylvie while Momma cooks breakfast. I don't think she can get along without me."

"She can for one morning, Lonnie."

I know homesickness when I see it because I used to be that way myself. The first time I spent the night with Richard I was five, and I kept going to the window to see the lights of our house across the street. I wondered what Mom was doing and what Dad was doing and what Ned was doing, and if Richard's mother hadn't coaxed me out of it I'd have run across the street to find out.

"It'll be morning before long, Lonnie," I said. "Why don't you turn on the light and read comics if you can't sleep, and when it gets to be the time your parents wake up, then you can go home. You don't want to go back in the dark."

He agreed, although he didn't look very happy about it, and I got out all my comics, even my very best ones, and stacked them up on the floor by his bed.

The lamp didn't keep me awake at all. When I woke up again it was full daylight and all the birds were singing.

The lamp was still on and most of the comics that had been on the floor were on the bed, but Lonnie wasn't there.

I told Grandma when I went downstairs that Lonnie had gotten a great urge to go eat breakfast in his own house.

"Well, well," Grandma said. "To each his own, I guess. He didn't know I was going to cook eggs and grits and sausage for breakfast."

I know it wouldn't have made any difference to Lonnie if he had known. He must have wanted to eat something that had the right taste to it.

I was fooling around in the front yard a little while later when Lonnie came down the road. He didn't mention breakfast, and I didn't either.

"We ought to go on over to Myra's and feed Wol," I said, and he agreed, so after I told Mom, we took off.

Myra was sitting in her backyard where you can see a little bit of the river through the trees. She was sitting out there trying to eat breakfast. I say *trying* because Willie was in her lap grabbing off little pieces of the roll she was eating and putting them in his own mouth.

"Sit down, boys, and I'll get you some tea," she said.

"I don't drink tea," I said quickly, but that didn't stop her. She dumped Willie in our laps and headed for the kitchen. Willie made angry little clicking noises and climbed down to follow her in that funny, wobbly way he walks.

Myra came back in a few minutes with a tray — a plate of rolls and butter and a jar of jam with a knife sticking in it and two mugs of tea. Lonnie and I sniffed the tea and made faces at each other.

"That's just green tea," Myra said, "and it won't do you a bit of harm. In fact it's good for your nerves, although I suppose at your ages you don't even know you have nerves."

I took a little sip of the tea and it sure wasn't very good. About like drinking boiled water.

"You ever drink sassafras tea?" Lonnie asked. "You have to dig up sassafras roots and boil them and then you drink the water. Thins down your blood after the wintertime. It doesn't taste any worse than this here."

"Bring me some roots next spring and I'll try it," Myra said. "Wherever Tremain and I lived I always made it a point to eat the native foods. I am a person who has lived everywhere and thrived."

"If you thrived in all those other places why did you end up here?" I asked.

"Because it's a beautiful place," Myra said. "Don't you think it's beautiful? Perfect if you could eliminate a few things. Or a few people, perhaps I should say. I like a hot climate. Love the heat like a lizard. And I've got the river practically at my back door and a wonderful variety of birds all year round. But of course there is a fly in the ointment."

"They been back?" Lonnie said. "Those people who shot your birds?"

"No. But I don't doubt they will be."

Willie had taken a roll from the plate and was sitting up on his haunches holding the roll in his paws and eating it just like a person.

"Don't think," Myra went on, "that I'm just a poor helpless little widow woman, as people around here say. I've got a rifle in my house and I know how to use it, but I've decided against that for the time being."

"You mean, you'd shoot them?" I said.

"Oh, for heaven's sake," Myra said. "Of course I wouldn't *shoot* them. Just give them a good scare is what I'm talking about."

I had a picture of Myra like Betsy in that song "Sweet Betsy from Pike." Shooting Indians from behind a covered wagon.

"It'd just make them worse," Lonnie said. "Just give them the excuse to cut loose, as my daddy would say."

"That's exactly the decision I came to myself," Myra said, putting down her mug with a thump and standing up.

We all went in the kitchen to get meat to feed Wol.

Myra made sure that the doors were shut and that Willie and Bertram were outside, because she said that we ought to give Wol a chance to fly and stretch his wings. When she lifted Wol out of the chest, Lonnie held out his finger for him and he clamped his talons around it right away, turning his head around so he could watch us. I could see why people talk about owls being wise, because Wol did have a calm, thoughtful look like he was thinking deep thoughts. Thoughts people probably wouldn't be smart enough to think.

Today his other eye was open — the hurt one — and as Myra said, it didn't look too promising. It was smaller than the other eye and darker. The black took up practically his whole eye, while the other one was nearly all gold colored.

"I don't think he can see a thing out of that eye today," Myra said. "Maybe it will get a little better in the next few days."

"Can an owl get along with just one eye?" I asked as I held out the first piece of meat to Wol.

"I just don't know," Myra said. "An owl needs to judge distance when he's hunting, but maybe he could learn to do that with one eye."

The piece of meat was bigger than Wol liked, so he shook it in his mouth and let it fall to the floor. When I held out a smaller piece, he took it right away and swallowed it. Then he leaned forward to watch me choose another piece. He was hungry and ate all the pieces that Myra had cut up for him except for the big one.

We offered him a drink, but he wasn't interested in water.

"I bet in the wild he gets all the water he needs from the blood of the things he catches," Lonnie said.

Wol was so gentle and so mannerly and civilized with us that it was hard for me to imagine him tearing apart mice, but of course he must've done it. It's the same, after all, with cats. They're sweet as pie most of the time. Still, I don't like that look they get on their faces when they're watching a bird they want to catch.

Myra said that Wol should fly, but the trouble was that Wol didn't want to fly. Lonnie waved his finger up and down and Wol flapped his wings trying to keep his balance. He didn't want to let go.

He did let go, finally, and flew lopsided with one wing higher than the other. He made it to the other side of the room, but he flew straight into one of the big kites and made it quiver. When he tried to fasten his talons in it he tore a whole piece out, and then he skitted down the wall trying to find something else to grab hold of. Lonnie picked him up and started him flying back across. This time he ran into the coffee table and only got halfway. He kept bumping into things, and even when he saw that he was about to fly into the wall and reached out his talons for one of the masks, he missed and went sliding down to the floor again.

I don't think he liked flying around at all. When

I finally picked him up from behind a big geranium pot he looked awfully little and bedraggled.

"Maybe we'll have to keep him after all," I said as I put him back in the chest. "It seems mean to make him fly when he doesn't even want to."

"This is just the first time," Myra said. "We have to give him his chance. It's no life living in a cage."

Maybe not, but I wasn't so sure that Wol would mind being a pet. He kind of liked it, as far as I could see.

On the way home all Lonnie could do was yawn. I knew why, of course, since he'd been awake practically the whole night.

"Would you come and spend a night at my house?" Lonnie asked as we walked along watching the heat dancing over the fields.

"Not tonight."

"Well, sometime."

"If your mother says it's OK." I don't like spending the night in strange houses.

So I wasn't exactly enthusiastic but what could I do? Lonnie had spent the night with me even though he hadn't liked it much.

"See you after a while," I said when we got to Grandma's house. I wanted to be by myself for now. I just wanted to lie on my bed and read and play with Bernie and think about things.

# Chapter

## 6

For several days Lonnie and I were pretty busy going over to Myra's and feeding Wol and watching him fly — he was getting better at it but not much. And one day Mom took me to town to buy new sneakers — two pair, just in case — and she and Grandma took Lonnie and me on to Turner's Lake for a picnic. The water in the lake was so warm it was about like being in a great big bathtub. We stayed in for hours until Grandma said we were going to turn to prunes if we stayed any longer. I was trying to teach Lonnie the crawl, but I guess I'm not a very good teacher. Lonnie didn't like putting his head under the water and he'd do it only about long enough to take one stroke. Then his head would pop up again, and he'd be doing the old dog paddle. It was discouraging. Mom kept telling me to remember how I'd learned to swim, but that wasn't much help either because it'd taken me quite a while at the YMCA. For a long time all we did was float around like logs in the Y pool, and then we floated and kicked, and then we floated, kicked, and waved our arms. But I didn't have the patience or the time to go through all that with Lonnie.

We kept pretty busy but there was bound to come a day when we didn't have anything to do. When that day came, we lay in the tree house looking up at the leaves, which weren't doing anything but hanging there.

"What do you want to do?" Lonnie said.

"I don't know. What do you?"

We looked at the leaves and blinked for another long time.

"OK, what we got to do is go spring those traps," Lonnie said, starting to sit up.

I groaned. "It's too hot, Lonnie." I just wanted to lie there with my eyes shut.

"No, we got to do it. I'm not about to give up, and we haven't been there in a couple of days. Come on, Ben."

He had to pull me up. I felt like something that had melted and stuck to the floor of the tree house. "I bet it's a hundred degrees," I said.

"Hundert and ten in the shade, but the Tarantula and the Red Chigger aren't going to be stopped by a little heat."

We were about the only things moving around

in the woods. Even the birds were keeping quiet. Just the old locusts sawing up and down. The only thing besides us dopey enough to be walking around was a terrapin rattling through the dead leaves. I picked him up and held him upside down in my hand — I like to see the way terrapins draw in their legs and head into their shells and shut everything up as tight as a drum with that noise like airlocks closing. That's really neat. But this terrapin looked mad about being picked up, and he kept waving his legs in the air and craning his neck up trying to turn himself over. He was so mad he did a pee in my hand and I had to let him go.

I thought maybe the Mannings would have moved their traps since the last time we'd been there but they hadn't. Or if they had, the new places looked like the old ones. All we had to do was find the marks on the trees. We sprang the first two traps the same as always — just ho-hum stuff — but when we came to the third one it was already sprung. I was scared there was going to be a half-dead fox in the trap, and if there was, how were we going to get it out? When we pushed back the weeds to look, our hearts were really hammering.

But there was nothing in the trap. Or, at least, no animal. Just a tuft of whitish hair.

We didn't expect to find any more of the traps sprung, but when we got to the last one and started poking around with our sticks, the weeds began to move and flutter. My stomach sort of turned over when I saw that, and I felt sick.

Lonnie got on one side of the trap and I got on the other and we started flattening down the weeds with our sticks; we were afraid to put our hands down there for fear we'd get bitten. When we'd pushed back the undergrowth, we crouched down and looked. At first all I could make out was a pointed face and black eyes. But then I saw the tail.

"It's a raccoon, Lonnie!" I said. "Just a raccoon."

We weren't scared of a raccoon so we pulled back the weeds to get a good look. The raccoon made those angry clicking noises like Myra's raccoon Willie made when he was mad about something. This raccoon was about Willie's size, too, which meant he wasn't grown yet.

"How are we going to get him out?" I asked.

"I guess we just pull the trap open. But how bad's he hurt? Can you tell?"

We could tell that his leg was scraped where the trap was holding it, but we couldn't tell if it was broken or not.

"What would Myra say if we brought her another raccoon to take care of?" I said. I could just see this one and Willie playing together. And maybe, just maybe, I could even take him home with me when I went. If I could talk Lonnie into that. And if I could talk Mom into it. I was already having an argu-

ment with Mom in my head about the raccoon sleeping in my bed with me.

But first we had to get him out of the trap.

"You do something with him at that end while
I try to open the trap," I told Lonnie.

"What do you mean, do something? Do what?"

"Oh, you know. Entertain him. Calm him down."

So Lonnie made whistling noises and wagged his
head up and down in the raccoon's face. But the raccoon wasn't a bit entertained, because he kept making
angry noises and trying to pull away.

I yanked on the trap, but it was harder to open
than I thought it would be. I really had to get my
shoulder into it and pull, and when the trap did open
it snapped open all of a sudden and I went backward
— heels over head.

When I got up, things were just the way I should
have expected. The raccoon had gotten out of the
trap as soon as it opened and was running off down
the creek bank.

"I tried to grab him but I couldn't do it," Lonnie
said.

The raccoon wasn't using his hurt leg, but he
was doing all right on the ones he had left, and he
disappeared into the bushes while we watched.

"His leg may not even be broken," I said. "And
think how glad he'll be to see his family again."

As soon as I imagined our raccoon running up to

his mother and brothers and sisters making those whistling noises raccoons make when they're happy, I thought how awful it would have been if the Mannings had found him, instead of us. They'd have clubbed him to death or shot him while he was stuck in that trap.

"I sure wish we could do something about Leroy and Butchie and those traps," I said.

"Like what?"

"How do I know like what? If I did, I wouldn't have to ask you, would I?"

Well, we stood there supposedly thinking, but it was too hot for me to think about anything except that we had a long walk home ahead of us.

"I got it," Lonnie said all of a sudden.

"What?"

"We'll tell the commandant of the army camp about Leroy and Butchie setting out traps and trespassing on army land."

"We trespass too every time we come here."

"That's different. We don't set out traps."

I felt weak in the knees. "What makes you think he'd believe us? He might not even let us in his office. We're just kids, Lonnie."

"Shoot, we can get in there some way. And look here. Don't you see what a good idea this is? Butchie and Leroy won't even know we're the ones who turned them in."

Well, I could see the beauty of that, all right. It

would be good to get revenge on them in a safe way.

"Well, how do we get to the army camp? It must be ten miles, and I'm not going to walk ten miles in this heat."

"Jesse'll take us," Lonnie said, looking pleased with himself.

So we went to Jesse's camp, woke him up from his afternoon nap, and told him we wanted him to take us to the army camp.

"What for? You planning on enlisting?" Jesse thought that was very funny, and he laughed until he went wheezy.

"We got business up there," Lonnie said.

"Oh! Business!" Jesse said. "Well, in that case I sure better get you there fast, hadn't I? I sure don't want to stand in the way of any business you may have with the U.S. of A. army."

"We have to turn somebody's name in," I said importantly. "Those Mannings have got traps set out on army land and we're going to turn them in."

"You right sure you know what you're getting yourselves into?"

"Sure as shootin'," Lonnie said.

Jesse shook his head. "All I know is that something that starts out looking plain as a pig's snout has a way of tangling itself up later on."

"Why should it?" I said.

All the way to the camp Jesse just kept shaking

his head like he was carrying on a conversation with somebody on the other side of the windshield and he disapproved of what the person was saying. "I'm going to let you all out here by the gate they keep closed," Jesse said to us. "If I take you to the big one they more'n likely won't let you in. In the meantime I'll just go on into town and buy myself some Black Mule chewing tobacker. When I come back by I'll park along right there in the shade. If anybody has anything to say about it, I'll tell 'em I'm letting my engine cool off. I'll just sit there till you show up. That sound all right to you?"

We nodded, and he stopped the truck and we slid out.

I don't know what it was, exactly, that got us under the gate and headed up the road that led to the barracks, but I've noticed this kind of thing happening before. Somehow your feet just go on and carry you, even those times when what you want more than anything else is to turn tail and run away like a three year old. It's the same when I have to go to the dentist. I want to run down those stairs from Dr. Henningham's office and keep right on going. But for some reason I don't do it. I sit there in the black chair with a bib around my neck watching the water run in that little white basin. I don't really know why, except, I guess, that there're just things you have to go on and live through.

"You scared, Lonnie?" I asked.

"Not much," he said, but when I looked over at him I saw he looked kind of pale, and he kept swallowing like somebody who's about to throw up.

There wasn't anybody else in sight. Just the heat waves making everything go wavy. Everybody at the army base could have fallen in a hole, by the looks of things.

When we finally got up even with the barracks, we saw some men playing baseball in a big, open space on our left, but they were a long way away and we didn't feel like walking all the way over there. I thought we'd be bound to find somebody handier to ask where the commandant was. The road made a turn and there was a long, low building in front of us with some cars and jeeps parked around it. In front there was a little bit of grass that somebody must've watered every night, it was so green, and there was a flagpole standing in the middle of it.

"You reckon that could be it?" Lonnie said.

"How would I know?" I said, feeling cross.

We lolled around outside, kicking the curb and trying to get up the courage to go into the building and ask about the commandant.

While we were standing there, a jeep slowed up and then stopped right beside us. We looked up and there was our old friend, Art, grinning and waving. "Hey," he said, "you couldn't be looking for me, could you? Hoping for some more comics or something like that?"

We shook our heads. "We're looking for the commandant of the base," I said.

Art looked surprised. "Think you might find him out here in the grass somewhere? Why in the world would you want to see him, anyway?"

I explained and Art whistled through his teeth.

"Well, if you really want to see him I'll take you to his office," he said. "His name is Colonel Wilcock. You got that? And he's not as bad as he looks, but he is what you might call overpowering."

"Scary?" I said.

Lonnie just stood there getting a silly look on his face. When I got the chance I intended to shake him.

"One of those no-nonsense types," Art said. "But you're not in the National Guard so what are you worried about?"

Plenty, I wanted to say. Plenty.

Art took us into the building and led us down a long hallway until we came to a room where there was a woman working at a desk. Art motioned for us to go and sit down on the slick-looking bench that sat against one wall while he talked to the woman. Twice he waved his arm toward us and the woman looked our way, so I knew Art was telling her about us.

After a while Art came over. "That's Colonel Wilcock's secretary and I've told her about you. She'll get you in to talk to him in a few minutes."

"OK," I said.

"Don't look so scared," Art said. "Just think: in thirty minutes it'll all probably be over."

"It may be all over, all right," I said gloomily.

Art just laughed and patted us on the shoulders.

When he left, we sat sticking to the bench and trying not to stare at Colonel Wilcock's door.

"You're not turning funny on me, are you, Lonnie?" I hissed to him. "Like you did that first time at Myra's. Because if you are, I'll kill you. Whose idea was this whole thing, anyway?"

I was just getting ready to give him a good kick in the ankle when the secretary motioned for us to come with her, and she took us into Colonel Wilcock's office.

Colonel Wilcock himself was sitting behind his desk — a very big man with a bald, shiny head and light blue eyes that kind of stuck out like a frog's. He just sat there, turning a pencil slowly up and down in his fingers and looking at us. I could tell he didn't think much of what he saw. I cut my eyes over toward Lonnie and saw what Colonel Wilcock must be seeing — a kid wearing dirty jeans and a shirt that was too little for him, sneakers with holes in them, and dried flakes of mud across his nose. I knew I didn't look any better. Why hadn't we at least washed our hands and tried to comb our hair? If my mother could see me at this minute she'd probably pretend not to know who I was.

I wondered if maybe we should salute Colonel

Wilcock, but since I didn't know the right way to do it I decided to let that pass. We just stood in the middle of the room, and we might have stayed there the rest of the afternoon if Colonel Wilcock hadn't spoken.

"Well?" he said. "What have you young men come to see me about? Don't just stand there with your tongues between your teeth."

I looked over at Lonnie and saw he was hopeless. He had that glazed look in his eyes, and I knew he wouldn't say a word. I wanted to kill him, but I couldn't do it right in front of Colonel Wilcock's desk.

When I tried to open my mouth, it seemed kind of paralyzed.

"Thraps," I said, finally. He was right. I *was* holding my tongue with my teeth.

"What did you say?" Colonel Wilcock said, looking fierce. "Speak up, boy. I can't stand mumblers."

"Traps!" I said, very loudly.

"Traps, is it? What about traps?"

"Somebody's - putting - some - out - in - the - camp - area," I said very fast. "Sir." I'd never called anybody *sir* before in my life but I suddenly remembered that soldiers were supposed to call officers that.

"And how would you know that?"

"We saw them. The traps, I mean."

"How do you come by this piece of information

unless you were there yourself? Unless, of course, you're leading me to believe you have second sight."

"We were looking for Lonnie's log," I said.

The colonel frowned and raised his eyebrows.

"Did I just say *log?*" I said, having a terrible sinking feeling that I had. "If I did, I meant *dog*. Looking for Lonnie's dog." The whole conversation was beginning to sound peculiar to me. I even forgot for the moment that we hadn't actually been looking for Lonnie's dog at all.

"So you were looking for Lonnie's lo . . . I mean, dog, and you came upon some traps. Is that what I'm to understand?"

I nodded my head.

"You two haven't been sent here on some kind of dare, have you?"

"Nobody could have dared us enough to get us to come *here*," I said.

Colonel Wilcock just sat there, turning the pencil in his fingers and looking at us so hard I thought he could probably see inside our heads. I thought it might look shifty if I looked down at the floor so I stared back at him, making my eyes go wide. I could feel Lonnie squirming beside me.

Colonel Wilcock put his pencil down on his desk with a thump. "If I send a man out with you right now could you take him to those traps so he can confiscate them?"

"Sure," I said, and then quickly added, "Yes,"

remembering that _sure_ wasn't what you were supposed to say when you wanted to be polite.

Colonel Wilcock went to the door and called out, "Send Sergeant Poole in here, please, Miss Cuthbert."

"It's Leroy and Butchie who're doing it," I said quickly because I was afraid I wouldn't get it in otherwise.

Colonel Wilcock looked back at me. "Repeat that," he said.

"Manning. I mean it's Leroy and Butchie who're doing it. Traps."

"Young man," Colonel Wilcock said, "is there something wrong with your tongue or is English not your native language?"

"Of course it is," I said indignantly. "I'm from Tarrytown, New York, and I've been an American all my life."

"Then use the language! Use it! What do you mean squawking to me like a sick chicken? And you," he said, turning to Lonnie. "Why are you squirming like that? If you need the bathroom it's down the hall and first door to your right."

"He doesn't!" I said, grabbing hold of Lonnie's arm and hanging on. Even if he didn't say a word, he was better than nothing. I'd as soon have been left in that room along with a wild lion as with Colonel Wilcock.

When Sergeant Poole came to the office, Colonel

Wilcock shook our hands and told us he wanted to see us in the military in about ten years' time. I didn't tell him so, but I pretty much made up my mind right then that army life wasn't for me.

As soon as we got out the door I gave Lonnie a sharp nudge in the ribs with my elbow to show him I was still mad at him. "Why didn't you say anything?" I whispered to him. "Why did you leave everything up to me?"

He just shrugged his shoulders.

"It'll be an icy day in August before I listen to you again, Red Chigger," I said.

"It all worked out, didn't it?" he said, as cocky as though he'd planned the whole thing in advance.

Things were looking good, I had to admit. Sergeant Poole took us off in his jeep and let us listen in on his walkie-talkie. All we had to do was take him out to the place where the traps were, help him get them back to the jeep, and ride back as far as the place where Jesse would be waiting for us. The Mannings would probably be afraid to put out any more traps in the camp, and they wouldn't even know that we were the ones who'd told on them. Easy as pie, it looked like.

I was feeling good when we led Sergeant Poole to the first four traps and he put them all out on the creek bank to pick up on our way out.

But to get to the fifth one, we had to follow a

bend in the creek, and when we came around that bend, there was a sight that made me go cold. Because right there in front of us, hunkering on their heels, were Butchie and Leroy! Butchie had a can of dog food in his hand, getting ready to empty it out for bait. But it wasn't the dog food I was looking at. All I could see was Butchie's face as he looked right straight at me, smiling the way a dog lifts his lips when he's thinking about biting. It was a look I'd just as soon forget.

They saw everything, of course, in a split second, so it wouldn't have done Lonnie and me any good to run. All it took was for them to see Sergeant Poole in his M.P. uniform and us beside him. Even a dimwit could have seen from that that they were in trouble and we'd gotten them into it.

Leroy and Butchie stood up very slowly, wiping their hands on the backs of their jeans.

"What are you doing there?" Sergeant Poole said.

"I reckon if you got two eyes in your head you can see what we're doing," Butchie said.

"You're going to have to come back to the base with me. Colonel Wilcock is going to want to talk to you. Right now you'd better show me where the rest of those traps are."

The three of them went on down the creek, but Lonnie and I headed the other way toward the jeep, picking up two of the traps to carry with us.

"They're going to kill us," I said. "They're just going to kill us, and we can't even do anything about it."

"Maybe they'll get put in jail for a long time."

"Do you think so?"

"Even if they do, they won't be in jail the rest of their lives, and who do you think they're going to get first when they get out? *I* have to ride the school bus with them."

"Maybe you can fight them off, Lonnie."

"Oh, sure, two against one."

"Well, to hear you talk sometimes, that wouldn't be any problem."

Sergeant Poole, Leroy, and Butchie came up out of the woods just then carrying the rest of the traps.

Leroy and Butchie walked straight over to where we were sitting by the jeep and dropped the traps they were carrying on our feet. We didn't even move. What could we do?

I was scared to look up, but I knew Leroy and Butchie were looking down at us. I felt about like a bug they were getting ready to step on. They were standing so close there was nowhere to look except at their jeans' legs. So I just looked straight ahead like that was a fascinating sight.

"They look kinda scared, don't they?" Butchie said. "Isn't that what you'd say? They look kinda scared? What'ja reckon they could be scared of? They hadn't done nothing they oughta worry about, have they?"

Leroy sniggered.

Lonnie and I didn't move a muscle.

Sergeant Poole didn't seem to notice any of this. He had other things on his mind, I guess. Five people and six traps to get in one jeep.

"We could just walk," Lonnie said, and Leroy sniggered again.

"I don't think they want to ride with us," Butchie said. "Is that the notion you get?"

"You just stay here, boys," Sergeant Poole said. "I'll get somebody to come and take you home while I take these two to the base."

He talked to somebody on his walkie-talkie and then they put all the traps in the back of the jeep and the three of them climbed in.

"Be seeing you," Butchie said to us, looking out the side of the jeep and grinning in a mean way.

We didn't wave back.

We didn't do anything except sit in the shade until another M.P. drove up in a jeep to pick us up.

He wasn't a very talkative soldier, but that was all right because we didn't feel like talking anyway. We told him where there'd be someone waiting for us in a truck, and he nodded his head. We rode on for quite a way without anybody saying a word, but finally I asked him the question that had been on my mind a long time.

"Those guys that got caught setting out traps on the army land," I said. "What'll happen to them?"

"Can't say," the soldier said. "Don't know the details."

"Well, but do you think it's likely they'll get sent to jail for a long time?"

"Oh, I wouldn't think so. No, just a good talking to from Colonel Wilcock is all I'd expect."

"That's all?" I said, feeling my spirits sink down past my feet. "They won't even get put in jail at all?"

"Not if it's a first offense. And it's not a very serious one."

I gave Lonnie a weak nudge and he nudged me back. We knew exactly what the other was thinking. If the soldier was right, Leroy and Butchie would be free by suppertime to start thinking about what they were going to do to us. I saw now what Jesse had meant by saying that things could get tangled up and turn out a lot different than what you expected. We'd gone through all that scariness of going to see Colonel Wilcock for nothing. Worse than nothing. There wasn't any way out of it that I could see. We were both going to get it.

# Chapter

## 7

I didn't say anything to Mom and Grandma about the trouble we'd gotten into. What was there to say? That Lonnie and I were going to be killed? If Ned had been there, I'd have told him, but since he was at that stupid camp he wasn't any use.

Lonnie and I stayed outside until nearly dark after Jesse brought us home. We sat in the dirt at the side of the road and talked about what we ought to do. It was another of those times I wished I really could be the Tarantula, leaping over the houses and trees to see what Leroy and Butchie were up to. Lonnie said maybe we should build ourselves a fort out of big rocks and just live in there except to come out to eat. We could keep a supply of weapons — slingshots and bows and arrows and just rocks to fight off Leroy and Butchie if they came around.

I shut my windows that night and locked them,

so my room got really hot and stuffy. Before I went to bed I sneaked downstairs and locked the doors, too. Half the time Grandma doesn't bother to lock doors; nobody ever comes out in the country to steal things. Before I went to sleep I strained my ears so hard I could just about hear Leroy and Butchie whispering around on the ground and climbing up the rose trellis.

The next day we stuck close to home and didn't even go to Myra's to feed Wol. We knew she wouldn't let him go hungry, but we were sorry to miss seeing him.

It was the middle of the afternoon before we even went as far as the tree house. Naturally we thought the tree house would be all right because it was back in the fields, not on the road at all.

Lonnie climbed up the ladder first and I'd just started when he yelled.

"What is it?" I said, climbing as fast as I could. When I scrambled onto the platform Lonnie was tugging at me and yelling for me to look. What I was supposed to look at was in plain sight: a sheet of paper nailed to the tree.

WE'RE GOING TO GET YOU, YOU LITTLE PIG SQUEALERS

That was all it said, but it didn't need to say anything else.

"Shoot fire!" Lonnie kept saying. "Shooooot fire!"

"Well, what're we going to do now?" I said, feeling doomed.

"Stay over at my house tonight," Lonnie said. "We'll fight 'em off together if they come after us."

I didn't think we could fight off the Mannings even if we were being Tarantula and Red Chigger, but it seemed to make sense that we should stick together. So I agreed to spend the night with him.

As soon as I got to his house late that afternoon Lonnie took me up to the room where he slept. It was a neat room because you got to it by climbing a ladder along the wall and it was about as close to a fort as you could get. Once you climbed up you could latch the trapdoor and there wasn't any other way in except two windows at either end, but they were high up. It was a big room with the chimney passing through. The roof came to a sharp peak up above and bunches of onions were hanging there drying out. The whole room smelled oniony, but it wasn't a bad smell.

"I never knew your house was a log cabin before," I said, looking around. You could see the logs with white plaster in the cracks. From outside it didn't look like logs because somebody had covered them over with boards.

"My great-granddaddy built it," Lonnie said. "He homesteaded and built this house himself."

I wanted to do more exploring, but there wasn't time because Lonnie's mother called us to supper.

Sylvie was already in her high chair, which was pushed up against the table, but when she saw me she started kicking her heels and saying "Hibo," all excited. I had to sit next to her so she wouldn't carry on. She stopped kicking her heels when I sat by her, but she leaned way over the tray of her high chair so she could look in my face. I felt silly saying "Hi, Sylvie" about every two minutes.

Lonnie's mom and dad thought it was funny the way Sylvie had taken to me, and Lonnie's dad kept saying, "Aren't you getting a little ahead of yourself, looking for a boyfriend?" to Sylvie, and she kept patting her hands at him. I felt embarrassed sitting there in the middle and I knew my ears were going pink.

Lonnie's mother started passing around the food, and since Lonnie was taking spoonfuls of everything I guessed I'd better take a little of everything too. Corn on the cob was all right, but fried okra! Ugh! I took about a teaspoonful of that and not much more of the black-eyed peas, and the smallest piece of meat I could see. It was dark brown and cut in little skinny pieces — chicken, maybe, or something like that. I could see I was going to be making most of my meal on corn, cornbread, and milk. But nobody's going to starve on that.

I discovered that Sylvie had a use, after all. She was nearly as useful as a dog. She thought it was a lot more fun taking food out of my plate than it was hers, and what she really liked doing was picking up peas or pieces of okra one at a time with her fingers. Just like a monkey. I scooted the peas and okra over to the edge of my plate so she could get them easier, and she finished them all.

I'd nearly finished eating the brown piece of meat when Lonnie's dad said, "Say, you kinda like fried squirrel, don't you? Help yourself to some more."

I shook my head and felt my stomach go all funny. Fried squirrel! I wouldn't have touched it with a ten-foot pole if I'd known. Fried squirrel was even worse than spinach pie. I gave Lonnie a dirty look, but how was he to know I didn't want to eat squirrel? I kept thinking about Myra's squirrel and feeling queasy.

I didn't recover until Lonnie's mom brought out a peach cobbler, hot from the oven, for dessert. The crust was pale brown and the juice from underneath had bubbled up over the edges. I nearly burned my tongue on the first bite, but even so I could tell it was really good. "This is even better than Grandma's," I said.

"Oh, your grandma's one of the best cooks around," Lonnie's mother said. Well, she is too, but that cobbler was really great.

Lonnie and I did the dishes after supper. I didn't mind doing them as much at his house as I do at home. We put two big dishpans on the table and heated water in a kettle on the stove, and it seemed more of a challenge or something to do them that way instead of in a sink. After we got them done, we drew water out of the well to fill the bucket so there would be water to make breakfast with. Then we went out on the front porch where everybody else was.

It was getting dark and the whippoorwills were calling and the katydids had started up. Lonnie's mom, dad, and Sylvie all sat in the swing, and Lonnie and I sat on the steps with Geronimo drooling on our feet.

"Tell a story, Daddy," Lonnie begged, but his dad put him off for a while, teasing a little bit exactly the same way Grandma teases about telling stories.

"You right sure you want a story?" Lonnie's dad said. "You won't get skeered in the dark if I tell you about haints and things like that?"

We shook our heads and even Sylvie said "Story" and clapped her hands.

So he started telling about things that had really happened to people who'd lived in the woods around about or up on Mulberry Mountain. Things his grand-daddy had seen with his own eyes. A haint that rose up every day just about dark and sat on the rail fence by the far pasture. He was wearing overalls and work shoes like anybody else, but you could tell he was a haint all right because his face looked terrible up close like a dead person's would, and you could see right through him like smoke. Well, he appeared there so often on the rail fence, same time every day — just about suppertime — that Lonnie's great-granddaddy got used to seeing him sitting there, and he got up the nerve one evening to call out to the haint, "What'd you want, anyways, sitting there on my fence ever night, haint?"

The haint looked right at him with its eyes like holes and its face white as could be. "I'm hongrey," the haint said.

After a few more days Lonnie's great-granddaddy got up the nerve to ask the next question. "What'd you want to eat, anyhow, haint?"

And the haint answered right up like he'd just been waiting for the chance. "Cornbread and cold buttermilk," he said.

Lonnie's great-granddaddy was bothered that there should be a haint sitting on his fence every night pining for buttermilk and cornbread, which were two things he and his wife had plenty of. He didn't know what anybody else would say about it, and he guessed they'd have discouraged him if they could, but the next night he didn't say a word to his wife. He just took a big glass of buttermilk and a piece of cornbread and a spoon out of the kitchen after supper when his wife had gone to the yard to sit in the cool. He carried those things and a long board out to the field where the haint was in the habit of sitting.

Sure enough, when Lonnie's great-granddaddy got to the field there was the haint looking hungry as ever. So he put the food and the spoon on the end of the board and held it out to the haint. He didn't want the haint's cold hand touching his. The haint took the buttermilk and the cornbread as polite as could be and crumbled up the bread in the milk and proceeded to eat it with a spoon the same as anybody else.

When he'd eaten every crumb he looked at Lonnie's great-granddaddy and said, "I shore am much obliged to you." He didn't look as terrible in the face anymore, and Lonnie's great-granddaddy thought that another glass of buttermilk might even bring a little color to the haint's white cheeks. However, the haint faded away, same as always, and although Lonnie's great-granddaddy came out every evening after supper looking for him, the haint didn't come back anymore. It wasn't until then that Lonnie's great-granddaddy heard about a poor old man who'd starved to death back in his cabin a few winters before that. Poor old man broke his leg and couldn't move and just lay there and starved, so it wasn't any wonder he kept coming back looking for some supper.

I didn't think that story was a bit scary, even if it was about a haint. The next one he told got to me more, somehow.

This one was about a man who'd lived over on the Mountain years ago. He fell in love with a girl who lived in one of the hollows round about. It looked like it would be a good match and everybody was all for it except for one person, and that was the man's mother. She was a widow woman who didn't have any children other than the man, and she didn't want him marrying and leaving home. She wouldn't even come to the wedding, but it took place anyhow, and the man and his wife moved into a house at the bottom of the Mountain. Things went along real well for a while and the man and his wife were very happy. But then a thing started happening that seemed a little peculiar. This old wild hog started coming out of the woods and making trouble for the man and his wife. They'd plant a garden, and the hog would come and root it up. It would pull clothes off the line and tear them with its tusks, but it always ran off into the woods before the man could get his gun and shoot at it. More than once when the man and his wife were sitting at the table eating supper, the hog would appear out of the woods and stand just where the darkness of the woods started, looking at the house with its little red eyes.

Well, one day the man had to go to market and he left his wife home all day by herself. When he came back late in the afternoon, his wife didn't come out to meet him. He called all through the house, but she didn't answer from anywhere. He was scared by this time and went running around the yard calling her name. It wasn't till he got to the garden that he saw her lying in a heap in one corner. She was dead as could be, and all around where she was lying there were the prints of a hog's feet. So the man ran into the house and got his gun and followed those prints the hog had made back into the woods. When he'd gone about halfway up the Mountain he came upon the hog itself. As soon as it saw him, it stopped running and faced him and he expected it to charge, but it just stood there looking at him. Sad looking, he thought, which wasn't the way you'd expect a wild hog to look. Even when he brought his gun up to his cheek the hog just stood there, not running or charging. There was something about it that the man didn't like the looks of, but after all, the hog had just killed his wife and he didn't see why he shouldn't shoot it. So he pulled the trigger and a mighty strange thing started happening. That hog started turning into a person right before his eyes. The hog just disappeared, and there was a person lying on the ground dead. And who do you reckon the person was? Why, it was his mother a lying there. It was his own mother with a bullet through her head.

When Lonnie's dad finished that story I felt the goose pimples rising on my arms. It was dark by this time and there were owls calling in the woods, maybe as far as Mulberry Mountain where the man had lived and where the Mannings lived now. If that man's mother could turn herself into a wild hog, who's to say that the Mannings couldn't turn themselves into wild animals too? I could just see them coming through the woods, red eyes shining in the dark, looking for us. I felt scared the same way I had once on a Boy Scout overnight when we stayed up late telling ghost stories. Nobody had wanted to go to our dark tents where things could be sitting waiting for us.

Now we had to go into Lonnie's house and head for bed. "Could we bring Geronimo to bed with us?" I asked Lonnie.

"How'd we ever get him up there? He's too heavy to get up the ladder."

Well, he was too; I could see that. But I sure wished we could've taken him to bed with us.

We climbed up the ladder, and Lonnie turned on the light. I didn't like the looks of things a bit. Before, I'd felt like Lonnie's room was a safe place. With the trapdoor latched, what could get us? But now I saw there might be things out there to be scared of that wouldn't be stopped by doors or even by walls.

We stripped to our underwear, Lonnie turned out the light, and we ran for the bed in the dark.

I didn't like the way the moonlight came through the windows and made squares and lines across the floor. Some kind of vine grew over one of the windows and the leaves moved and all those patterns on the floor moved too. And another thing. The roof of Lonnie's house was sheet iron and every little thing that touched it sounded like somebody was tapping on it with their fingers one place and then another.

"You don't believe that about people turning to wild hogs, do you?" I whispered to Lonnie.

"Naw."

"If Leroy and Butchie *could* turn themselves into something, what do you think it'd be?"

"Great big dogs. Black dogs with light-colored eyes."

"Yeah, that's what I think too," I said, my heart beating fast. When I closed my eyes I could see them loping through the woods side by side, their tongues hanging out and their eyes like foxfire.

I slept, but after a while I woke up and opened my eyes. It was still night and the moon was making everything look eerie. I was afraid I needed to go to the bathroom, but I tried to put that thought out of my mind because there isn't a bathroom in Lonnie's house. You have to go outside to the outhouse, and there was no way I was going to get out of that bed in the dark and grope my way down the ladder and through the house and then outside in the moonlight to that dark outhouse where anything could be waiting.

I was thinking about this and telling myself I didn't need to go to the bathroom after all, when somewhere out there in the moonlight Geronimo started howling. That's an awful noise to hear in a strange, dark room in the middle of the night. It's a mournful noise but wild and scary too, and all the little hairs on my arms started rising. It made me think that Geronimo was talking to all those haints that probably came out in the woods at night. If anything could, that noise could call up strange animals that spent their days being people.

I pulled the sheet right over my head and pushed up against Lonnie until he started kicking me in his sleep.

I slept again but when I woke up, my head was still under the sheet. Geronimo had stopped howling and everything seemed quiet.

But it wasn't. Because I started hearing this noise like somebody whistling a very high-pitched whistle.

I reached up and pulled the sheet down very slowly until I could see out. As soon as I did that some black, shadowy thing flew right over my face, practically grazing my nose. I went back under the sheet and started thumping Lonnie.

"There's something in here with us," I said.

"In the bed?"

"Out *there!* Can't you hear that whistling?"

We held our breaths.

"Yeah. I hear it."

"There's a black thing. Flying around."

Lonnie peeked out of the sheet, but all of a sudden he ducked back down.

"It's a bat," he whispered. "That thing nearly got my face."

"He did that to me too. You don't think that

could be a vampire bat, do you? Aiming for our throats?"

"Oh, lordy," Lonnie said.

"Another thing," I said, whispering real soft. "You don't think Leroy and Butchie could've turned themselves into bats and come in here after us, do you?"

If it hadn't been for the moonlight and Geronimo howling and that story Lonnie's daddy told I never would have had a thought like that. But as it was, it seemed reasonable enough.

"I don't know," Lonnie whispered back.

"We got to get out of here."

"How're we going to do that with that thing out there?"

"We got to keep under cover. We'll have to keep the sheet over us and go to the door that way."

So we pulled the top sheet off the bed and kept it over us while we slid down to the floor.

"Keep down," Lonnie said. "We don't want that thing flying into us."

That seemed like a good idea, but it was hard to crawl across the floor under the sheet. "Stop *pulling* on it, Lonnie," I told him. "My feet are already out there in the open."

"He's not going to fly down and bite your feet," Lonnie said, his voice muffled in the sheet. "It's your head you've got to worry about."

I was worried about my head, but I was worried

about the rest of me, too. And it seemed like we'd been in that sheet a long time just inching our way across the floor. It was as dark as a giant's pocket in there.

"You don't even know where we're going," I told Lonnie. "We's just going around in a circle, I bet."

"Listen here, I could find my way across my own floor tied up in a tow sack. You think you could do any better?"

"Ouch!" I said. "I *know* that's the second time I've come down on that same marble, unless you have marbles all over the floor."

I kept thinking about Amundsen at the South Pole and how his men could get lost in the swirling snow two feet outside their tents. I figured Lonnie and I were going to crawl around there in the dark for hours and hours while that bat dive-bombed us like a fighter plane.

"Got it!" Lonnie said all at once. "Trapdoor latch."

I couldn't see a thing until Lonnie swung back the door, and then I could see the black hole where the ladder was.

"You go on down first," Lonnie said. "But don't pull the sheet off me."

I had to go down by feel; couldn't see a thing. When I was nearly to the bottom I stepped on a piece of the sheet, slipped, and went falling to the floor. Then Lonnie fell on top of me, and we were all mixed up in the sheet and yelling, and I kept shouting to shut the door because I was scared that bat was going to follow us out the trapdoor.

Lonnie's mom and dad came running and turned on the light and untangled us. When we told about the bat, Lonnie's dad climbed up the ladder to shoo it out the window; then Sylvie woke up and started crying, and Lonnie and I were left standing under the light, blinking, and feeling kind of silly. With the light on I knew that bat up there was just a little fruit bat and not a vampire or a person changed into a bat. I got Lonnie to come with me, and we went to the outhouse.

It was pale grey outside and not black anymore. The air was soft, and a screech owl — just like Wol, I guess — was finishing up his hunting somewhere off in the woods and heading for home. Geronimo came out from under the house and walked along with us, bumping against our legs.

When we got back to the house, Lonnie's dad had shooed the bat out the window and shut it again and everything was OK. We went back to bed and to sleep, but it wasn't a very good sleep because I kept dreaming I was already awake and late for school, and Richard was calling for me out on the sidewalk. And I couldn't find anything — my shoes, or my sweater, or my books, or anything. I don't know why I should have dreamed a thing like that.

# Chapter

# 8

It's a funny thing about being worried about something the way Lonnie and I were worried about Leroy and Butchie. If nothing happens for a while, you put the worry out of your mind; you just can't keep up thinking about something like that twenty-four hours a day.

Since a couple of days went by and we didn't see Leroy or Butchie and didn't get any more messages from them, we stopped thinking so much about them. And we did have Wol to think about. He was changing practically every day. Now when we came into the room to feed him we could hear him thumping around in the chest even before we opened it, and when we did and one of us put his hand in the chest, Wol would clamp his talons around a finger. We'd lift him out and he'd turn his head, looking at us like he was saying, "Well, where's breakfast? Which one of you is going to have the sense to stop staring and get down to business?"

When we held out pieces of meat to him he didn't bother staring at them the way he had in the beginning, trying to figure out, maybe, what kind of a peculiar animal he was being offered to eat. He just snatched the piece of meat off our fingers, and he wasn't nearly as well mannered as he used to be. We didn't have to make him fly, either, shaking him off our finger the way we had in the beginning. As soon as he'd had enough to eat he'd just spread his wings and take off. He hardly ever bumped into things now and it got harder and harder to catch him to put him back in the chest.

One morning we got to Myra's and found her sitting in the yard writing in her bird book. "Peculiar thing happened last night," Myra said after we sat down. "Wol had a caller."

"A visitor?" I said, sitting down on the grass. I had this crazy picture in my mind of an owl knocking on the door with its beak and saying to Myra when she opened the door, "Can Wol come out and play?"

"I woke up in the night and heard a commotion of some kind taking place on the porch. I thought that some animal was after Willie, and he'd taken refuge there. You know the way he opens the screen door anytime he wants to. So I grabbed the broom as I went through the kitchen in case I had to fight some animal away. I turned on the porch light but there didn't seem to be anything there. Willie was nowhere in sight, although the screen door was wide open. But then I heard a fluttering among the plants. And when I looked up, there was an owl hanging on to a flowerpot."

"Screech owl?" Lonnie asked.

"It certainly was. It looked exactly like Wol. In fact, it was uncanny. I thought at first it *was* Wol, and he'd gotten out of the chest somehow. But then I remembered that Wol only had one eye and this owl had two. Great big yellow eyes looking at me. I stared at him and he stared at me and then he spread his wings and sailed out the door like some shadow taking off."

"Do you reckon he came for Wol?" Lonnie asked. "That they were friends and he was coming to get Wol to go off with him?"

Myra shook her head. "Owls live solitary lives most of the time. I think it was one of two things. Either the owl was looking for a mate or it was warning Wol to stay off its territory."

"But how did that owl know Wol was here?" I asked. "He's been inside the house ever since we brought him over. Unless that owl saw him in the parakeet cage and has been hanging around ever since." But I couldn't quite imagine an owl doing that — waiting around for so long. "And Wol's never made a sound that I've heard. Not since we got him."

"Maybe he makes noises we can't hear," Lonnie said. "Noises that just other owls can hear."

"I think that could be it," Myra said.

Wol was wilder that day than I'd seen him before. He took off to fly around the room when he'd eaten only a few pieces of meat, and he spent about fifteen minutes flying back and forth between the New Zealand mask and a picture frame on the other side of the room. Every time he'd land on one of those and we'd climb on chairs and try to grab him, he'd take off for the other one. When we separated — Myra over by the picture frame and Lonnie and I by the mask — Wol landed on the chandelier in the middle, starting it to sway and make little tinkling noises. He kept turning his head to keep up with what we were doing. He wasn't any dummy. I didn't think we'd ever catch him again, but after we'd chased him around for quite a while, he got flustered and landed on the floor between the wall and the big geranium pot where Lonnie was able to grab him.

We put Wol back in his chest and sat down to rest. We were red in the face and sweaty from all that running around.

"I'm too old to go through that every day of the week," Myra said. "We are going to have to let him go."

"He still hasn't got but one eye," Lonnie said.

"That didn't bother him much just now," Myra

said. "And I don't see why it should in the wild, either."

"Maybe it's different in the wild," I said. "Maybe he'll starve to death out there."

I couldn't make up my mind what I thought about it. I knew Wol wanted to be a wild owl again, and I couldn't blame him for that. Who'd want to live in a chest all the time when he had wings and talons like Wol's? He could sail through the night on those wings that were quieter than the wind and have all the woods and hills and river for his own. I understood that. But alongside of that picture in my mind was another one. In it, Wol was sitting dejectedly in a tree with his feathers all fluffed out around his neck the way they were the first day we found him. Every day he would get weaker and weaker until he'd finally just fall out of the tree and something would eat him.

"I wish there was somewhere like a very, very good zoo where he could go to live and have a big place to fly around in and still be fed," I said.

"There's no place like that around here," Myra said. "But when we turn him out, we'll put some meat in a tree nearby, and if he can't find anything else to eat maybe he'll remember the meat and come back for it. We'll check every day."

"All right," I said, feeling a little better.

Even if I hadn't been convinced by Myra I guess I would have been the next day, because when we came to feed Wol he was fluttering around in his chest, and when we took him out we could see that the tips of his wings were getting frayed.

"He's going to ruin his wings if he keeps doing that, and then he can't fly a-tall," Lonnie said.

I knew that was the truth, so when Myra said we should let him go late that very afternoon I agreed. "You boys can stay and eat with me and I'll take you home afterward," Myra said.

I guess she wanted it to seem like a party, but I didn't feel very happy when Lonnie and I went back to Myra's house later. I had that queasy feeling in my stomach I get when I've got to go to the dentist. I kept saying to myself that I ought to be glad for Wol, going back to the woods and maybe seeing other owls he knew again. But this didn't really cheer me up. Come to think of it, it was just the way I felt when we left Ned at that summer camp. I knew he wanted to go to camp, but I still felt terrible when we drove away and I looked back and saw him standing in the middle of the driveway, waving.

I opened the chest and took Wol out, and he was just as gentle and quiet as could be. He kept looking around at me with his one golden eye, and I thought he looked expectant and hopeful, like maybe he was thinking, could it be? Could it be what I'm hoping for?

"Let's turn him loose down by the river," Myra said. "That's the wildest and best protected spot there is on my land."

So we trooped out — Myra ahead carrying the meat for Wol in waxed paper, Lonnie and I side by side taking turns carrying Wol, and Willie coming along behind complaining. He didn't want to be left behind, but he wished somebody would pick him up.

I carried Wol first, and as soon as I went outside I could feel him getting tense between my hands. He didn't struggle, but he kept looking around and he got very alert. He knew where he was, all right, even if the last time he'd been outside he'd been in a parakeet cage. He knew he was close to home and freedom. I knew how he felt because when I get close to home after being away for a while I notice every tree, and I want to be sure that nothing's changed since I left.

To get to the river, we had to cross Myra's backyard and go down a steep, woody bank. I was holding Wol in my hands and sliding down the bank when he made a funny little trilling noise. "Hey, Wol just said something," I called out to Myra.

"Poor little fellow," Myra said. "Shut up in a chest for days. No wonder he's happy now."

But it made me feel sad for some reason — Wol had probably never been happy with us. All the time he'd been thinking about the woods.

When we got to the bottom of the bank, we stopped a few feet away from the river, where the water was flowing along pretty fast, but without making a sound. The woods were thick all along the bank and it looked like a good place to turn an owl loose.

We argued about where to leave the meat, and all the time Wol was craning his head around looking at everything. Lonnie favored hanging the pieces of meat on twigs and I wanted them put together in a pile. We finally decided on a willow tree that had a flat branch where I put some of the meat, and Lonnie hung a few pieces on twigs too so it looked like Wol couldn't miss it. Lonnie held him up to the meat, but I'm not sure he saw it. He was too excited.

We all patted him on the head one last time for luck, and then it was time to let him go.

Lonnie set him in the tree by the meat. Wol sat there for a minute, ruffling up his feathers because they'd gotten slicked down from our sweaty hands. Just before he raised his wings and took off, he looked at us with his one golden eye, and then he was flying, making for the top of the tallest tree around. "Goodbye, Wol!" Lonnie and I shouted like idiots, waving our hands. He didn't look around again. He just landed in the tree, swaying up there and getting his bearings, and then he took off again, heading west where the sky was yellow from the sunset. I felt proud of him up there flying so well and not bumping into trees.

We didn't say much as we climbed back up the bank, and it was a relief when we came across Willie halfway up. He was huffy because nobody had carried him and he'd missed out on whatever had been going on. Myra carried him the rest of the way, and he looked over her shoulder the way a baby does.

When we got back to the house Myra let Lonnie and me feed Willie while she cooked. Willie followed us around the kitchen, watching us get out his puppy chow and pour it into a bowl. He didn't eat puppy chow the way a dog would. He picked up the bowl with his front paws and sat on his haunches eating one piece of chow at a time. When he'd finished that, Myra said we could give him a banana. We loved giving Willie bananas. He peeled them just like a monkey and scooted away if you came close, because he didn't want to share his banana with anybody else.

Myra was one of those grown-ups who don't believe in having children sit around being idle. After we fed Willie, she gave us a bowl full of water and something that looked like pieces of paper rolled up into tiny balls. "Just drop those in the water and see what happens," she said. "Tremain and I got them in Hong Kong a long time ago and I've never had the occasion to use them. Tonight's just the right time, I think."

So we dropped a couple of the little balls in the water, and as they settled to the bottom they started loosening and opening out. Before they got to the bottom they'd turned into flowers. Mine was a white water lily and Lonnie's was a pink one. We had the bowl full of flowers by the time Myra said we should put it in the middle of the table and sit down to eat.

I couldn't believe what Myra set on the table for us to eat. A great big, round, beautiful pizza! A sensible one, too, with sauce and cheese on one half and sausage on the other. No anchovies or mushrooms. "How did you know pizza's my favorite?" I said. It was the first pizza I'd had since I left home. "Do you like pizza as much as I do, Lonnie?"

"Sure," Lonnie said.

"I'd probably die of indigestion if I shared it with you," Myra said. "I'm having cheese and biscuits and tea myself, but I'm delighted if you're happy."

"After weeks of just having stuff that's good for you," I said. "Boy!"

"There's some absolutely revolting-looking ice cream for dessert. Marshmallow chocolate or some such thing."

"Great!"

"Oh, I may be a crazy old woman but I know a thing or two about boys."

She was right. I loved eating at Myra's because when Willie climbed up in a chair and begged for pieces of pizza, she gave him a plate and let him eat like a human; then Bertram was afraid he was missing out, so he climbed up on the table with a nut in his mouth and proceeded to eat it right there, whisking his tail over our plates. When Willie went from the chair to the table and washed his paws in the bowl of flowers, Myra said we might as well leave the table to the animals and take our ice cream into the living room and try to eat in peace.

It wasn't peaceful for long, though, because Willie followed us and insisted on sitting in a lap. We were laughing and trying to finish our ice cream, when suddenly I heard a screech owl out in the woods somewhere.

We all got quiet and listened. Of course I hoped it was Wol, but there was no way of knowing. After all, Wol had never made his hunting call when he was with us.

Even after we couldn't hear the owl any longer we were quiet.

"It's always hard letting things go," Myra said. "Of course you worry, but you have to do it anyway. Look at Willie. Next spring he'll want to go off and find a mate and live the wild life, and I'll have to let him go. He'll be in more danger in some ways than Wol, with those awful Manning boys quite capable of shooting him just for the fun of it."

When Myra drove us home that night I had it in my mind to tell her all about how Lonnie and I had gone to Colonel Wilcock and told on the Mannings, and how we were afraid they'd take revenge on us. But, somehow, I didn't do it. You have to depend on your own wings sometimes the way Wol was doing, even if your flying can land you in trouble.

# Chapter

## 9

In the middle of the next afternoon, Lonnie and I decided we ought to go check on the meat we'd put out for Wol to eat. If any of it was gone we'd put out more. Of course, even if it was gone it didn't necessarily mean that Wol had eaten it — a shrike might have or even somebody's cat. But we decided we'd put out more anyhow on the chance that Wol was still depending on that meat for food.

Mom was in the house somewhere, and I did think about shouting to her to tell her where we were going, but I just didn't. We weren't going to be gone long — just over to Myra's to check on the meat and then right back.

We'd gotten in the habit of leaving Geronimo behind when we went to Myra's because he made Willie nervous, so we didn't whistle him up. All he ever did was to amble over in Willie's direction and sniff him, but Willie thought he was dangerous and would scold and look for something to climb on.

Anyway, we went by ourselves. Myra wasn't home when we got there, so we decided to go down to the river. We scrambled down the bank to the willow tree where we'd left the meat. It hadn't been touched as far as we could see, but it'd turned dark colored and it was a little shriveled.

I didn't know whether to be glad or sorry the meat was still there. It might mean that Wol hadn't eaten it because he didn't need to. Or it could just mean that he'd never really noticed it to start with.

Since there wasn't anything for Lonnie and me to do, we started walking along the river bank, throwing rocks in the water and looking up at the trees in case we might see Wol.

"Hey," Lonnie said suddenly. "Look at that."

There was a rowboat pulled onto the bank and tied up to a tree. It was one of those lightweight aluminum boats and we figured it must be Myra's since we were still on her land.

"She probably uses it for going down the river looking for birds," I said. She'd never mentioned having a boat before, but there was no reason why she should have. We climbed in it and sat for a while, pretending we were going on a trip down the river.

"We could just try it out," Lonnie said. "Just a little way along, sticking right by the bank."

"Oh, no, Lonnie," I said. "You're not going to get me out on that river in a boat."

"You scared?"

"Of course I'm not scared, but my mother would have a fit. So would yours."

"Shoot. We can take care of ourselves."

To tell the truth, I thought we could too. I had done some canoeing in scouts, and a canoe is harder to manage than a rowboat. But still I climbed out of the boat, and Lonnie climbed out with me.

Nonetheless, on our right a little way ahead there was this island, and we kept looking at it. It had a little sandy beach and trees in the middle. That island was just the right size for the two of us, and I knew we could have a lot of fun on it.

We were looking at the island when a big bird went sailing across the water to it and landed on one of the big trees in the middle.

"Say, did you see that?" I said to Lonnie. "Didn't that look like an owl to you?"

"I think it was Wol."

Well, if it was Wol it was our duty, practically, to investigate. We had to see if he looked OK.

"We could take the boat to get over there," Lonnie said.

"We won't have it very long. All we have to do is row over there, look at that bird, and row back."

So we ran back to the boat, untied it, and put it

in the water. I told Lonnie to sit still when we got in the boat and not go jumping around.

"Who're you telling about how to sit in a boat?" Lonnie said, looking mad. "You ever rowed a boat before?"

"I have a canoe and that's harder than a rowboat."

"Well, I have rowed a rowboat, so don't you tell me what to do. You take that oar and I'll take this one."

We sat side by side on the seat and tried to put our oars in the water at the same time and pull them together, but it was harder than it looked.

"This is the way to do it," Lonnie said, sounding self-important. "You put your oar in and pull back smooth, like this."

I tried, but my strokes were shorter and choppier than Lonnie's, so the boat sort of wobbled through the water. Instead of heading straight for the island, we were sidling along toward it.

"Just watch me," Lonnie said. "Shoot, it's easy as cutting butter with a spoon."

"If you don't stop acting like you know everything, I'm going to take my oar out of the water and hit you with it," I told him, and he looked a little surprised.

"You're the one's always going on about what a good swimmer you are and all that stuff. You brag a lot more than I do."

I wasn't sure this was true, but I didn't want to sit out there in the middle of the river arguing about it. "Okay, we're even," I said. "Let's just row."

Then Lonnie started counting: one, two, *three,* four, five, six. One, two, *three,* four, five, six. We put our oars down at *three* every time, and that worked a little better.

One good thing was that although we were pulling upstream the current wasn't as strong as it might have been because the island was a protection.

When we got to the island we pulled the boat up on the beach and left it there. It seemed like a safe-enough place; this wasn't the ocean, after all, where a wave could come and carry our boat away.

We didn't waste any time heading straight for the middle of the island where we'd seen the bird land. The island wasn't very big, and there was a path going through the little thicket of willow shoots and leading to the big trees in the middle. We walked around them, craning our necks and winking against the sun, but we couldn't see any birds sitting up there. Maybe ours had already left, although we hadn't seen any bird fly away.

We walked over to the other side of the island where we could see the wide part of the river. There was the other bank, quite a way over there, and we could see up the river for a long stretch. We were kicking rocks and fooling around when Lonnie nudged me with his elbow and pointed.

It was a dead tree, practically in the water, and there was a bird sitting on a branch. It could be an owl, but since its head was turned away, I couldn't get a good look.

"It *could* be him," I whispered to Lonnie as we tiptoed closer to the tree. We were underneath when the bird turned its head and looked down at us. As soon as it did that it lifted its wings and sailed out, heading back toward the land.

One glimpse was all we needed — there couldn't be but one owl with a single eye.

"It's him!" we yelled, running behind the owl to the end of the island. We jumped up and down yelling "Wol! Wol!" but of course Wol just kept right on flying. I guess we looked silly jumping up and down and yelling and waving at a bird, but there wasn't anybody around to see, except some people in a boat upstream, and they were too far away to tell what we were doing.

Now that we'd seen Wol, there wasn't any hurry to get back. Since we were on the island, we thought we might as well explore it. We went back to the middle where the trees were, and we found a place where people had been camping. A ring of rocks showed where they'd had a fire, and the usual stuff was scattered around — a bread wrapper, wads of aluminum foil, Coors beer and Pepsi-Cola cans. Between two trees we found some cord strung up for a clothesline and two tent pegs in the ground. We poked around hoping to find something really interesting such as some money or a knife but we didn't.

"You reckon your mother'd let you camp here overnight?" Lonnie asked. "Wouldn't that be fun?"

I thought it would. There's something special about an island, not like just sleeping out in the woods somewhere. It'd be more of an adventure on an island.

We were talking about tents and whether we'd need one or not, and we weren't paying much attention to anything around us as we headed back across the island through the thicket of willow trees. But on the other side, when we came to the beach where we'd left the boat, we stopped dead in our tracks.

Because, let me tell you, there was a sight that would curdle your blood.

Our boat wasn't on the beach. It was already several yards offshore — the gap widening every second — being towed along behind another boat, and in that one, grinning like apes, were Leroy and Butchie Manning.

We just stared at them with our mouths open, unable to say "Stop!" or "Come back!" or anything else.

Butchie put his hands around his mouth and yelled, "Cry for your mommas, you little squealers. They can't hear you if you yell so much your tonsils fall out, and we're not going to tell anybody where you are. Good-bye, squealers."

"Better not cry up a storm," Leroy said. "You're

on an island to start with and you might drown yourselves."

We sat there at the edge of the willow thicket
and watched them row off with our boat. What else
could we do? There wasn't anything to say. After a
while they passed a bend in the river and we couldn't
see them anymore.

"How'd they even know that was our boat?"
Lonnie said.

I'd already figured that one out. "They were in
that boat we saw up the river a while ago. You know.
When we were jumping around on the beach."

"Oh, boy," Lonnie said, shaking his head.

"I knew we shouldn't have come," I said. "I
shouldn't have listened to you."

"Shoot, you wanted to come over here as much
as I did."

He was right, but I sulked for a little while,
throwing rocks in the water and feeling mad at Lonnie. Then I saw there wasn't any use in keeping it up.
I _had_ wanted to come, and anyway we were stuck
there together, so it wouldn't help if I went on being
mad at him. After all, it would have been all right if
the Mannings hadn't happened to have been out
on the river on this particular afternoon — and if
they hadn't seen us on the beach. But they had been
there, and they had seen us, and that was all there
was to it. They sure must've laughed when they saw
what they could do to us.

"What do you reckon'll happen now?" Lonnie said.

I looked down at my watch and it said seven minutes after four. "They won't even start looking for us until five-thirty or six," I said. "Our mothers'll just think we're playing somewhere and they won't get worried until six-thirty or even seven. It'll take them that long to see we aren't any of the usual places. I'll bet they don't start really looking for us before seven-thirty, and then it won't be long until dark."

"Yeah," Lonnie said gloomily. "We better just hope somebody comes by in a boat before then."

"They could, couldn't they?" I said, feeling a little bit better. After all, it stood to reason that in the next three hours somebody would come by in a boat.

We decided to go to the tip of the island so if anybody came either side we'd be sure to see them. We started out feeling hopeful, but as the sun got lower and the shadows longer we started to worry. "This is a good time to go fishing," Lonnie kept saying. "Why isn't there anybody out there trying to catch some?"

I guess it just wasn't a night people were planning to eat fish for supper. There wasn't a house in sight on that part of the river; maybe that was the trouble.

After we'd been sitting there a long time without anything to look at except gnats dancing around in the sunshine and the river flowing along and the woods on the other side, I saw that we'd better try to make other plans.

"Lonnie, why don't you go scout all over the island and see if we might've overlooked something that would be useful. Like a fishhook maybe. Dry wood for a fire. Anything. We could be here all night. I'll stay and watch."

So Lonnie went off and he was gone a long time. The shadows were long — I looked at my watch and saw it was nearly six — and I was starting to get really hungry. Somehow I had a picture in my mind of a big ice chest sitting under a tree with sandwiches inside wrapped in waxed paper and still a little cool from melting ice. And there were cans of root beer and a package of potato chips and a bowl of deviled eggs. I could see it all so clearly in my mind that I thought the ice chest must be back there sitting against a tree. I must've seen it without noticing. I even knew which tree . . .

Lonnie flopped down on the sand beside me, and when I looked over at him, I knew he hadn't found any picnic chest full of food. His face had gone red, and sweat had made two tracks down his cheeks like he'd been crying. He rubbed his face in the crook of his elbow and shook his head.

"I even looked in all those little willow trees along the bank thinking somebody might've got a fishhook caught in there and lost it, but I couldn't find *anything.* I mean nothing. No fishhooks. No matches somebody might've dropped. Not a thing in the world."

My heart sank down to my toes.

"What're we going to do, then?"

"I been thinking," Lonnie said. "Maybe we ought to swim back."

Well, we walked over to the side of the island toward the shore and looked. It wasn't all that far. If it'd been a lake I'd have done it in a minute. But this was a river and there were those currents and undertows to worry about. And I knew how Mom had always said to Ned and me that we were not ever, ever to go swimming in the river no matter how hot the day was.

"We might do it as a last resort," I said. "But you can't swim all that well, Lonnie, and I don't know whether I could get both of us across or not."

"If you can get over there, I can too," Lonnie said, sticking out his bottom lip in that way he has when he thinks he's being insulted. But neither one of us was ready to go jumping in the river right then and there. The sun was going down, and the water looked dark.

"Shoot. I could eat a horse," Lonnie said, rubbing his stomach.

"I feel like that ghost in the story your dad told."

We weren't hungry enough to eat leaves, though, and there wasn't anything else.

We were standing there by the edge of the water listening to our stomachs growl, when we suddenly heard a loud throbbing noise in the air. A helicopter. "Where?" Lonnie said, turning around in a circle staring at the sky, which was all light and clear the way it is after the sun's gone down but before it's gotten dark.

"There it is!" I said. The helicopter was heading down the river, not passing over the island at all, but we ran anyway as fast as we could to the other side of the island. We started waving our arms and yelling, but the helicopter had already passed the island and was going on. An army helicopter. We watched it until it was just a speck, and then I blinked my eyes and lost it.

"Even if they saw us they'd think we were playing," I said. It seemed somehow lonelier on the island after the helicopter passed out of sight. Then, too, there was another reason it seemed awfully quiet and lonely all of a sudden. Soon it would be dark.

"We've got to make a fire now before it gets dark," I said.

I hadn't thought of it before, how dark it was going to be without a flashlight or anything. I guess Lonnie hadn't thought about it either because he ran around just as crazy as I did looking for dry leaves and sticks and all that. We dragged up a couple of dead tree limbs and broke them in pieces and made a stack of all this stuff in the fireplace the campers had left.

"Do you know how to get a fire going with two rocks?" I asked Lonnie. We were both kneeling by the rocks and looking down at that dry wood like we expected magic to light it up for us.

"Shoot, no," Lonnie said. "I never even saw anybody make a fire like that. Did you?"

"I saw some Indians once on television making fire, only they had a stick they turned fast between their hands."

We got two rocks and hit them together every way we could think of until our hands hurt, but not a thing happened.

"I thought you're always bragging about how you're a Boy Scout," Lonnie said, rubbing the rocks back and forth like he was playing cymbals.

On the other side of the fireplace I was trying that business with the stick, but all I know is that Indian must've had some trick up his sleeve I didn't know anything about. "You're the one always going on about how much you know about snakes and all that. To hear you talk you'd think you were a regular Daniel Boone."

We glared at each other across the fireplace. We were both in a mood to get mad, but there was one thing that stopped us. We were both going to be in the dark soon if we didn't get that fire going, so we went on chunking those rocks together and turning that stick.

"Oh, shoot!" Lonnie said after a while, and threw his rocks into what would have been our fire if we'd gotten one going. "My hands are about to fall off."

When I looked up, I saw that it was so dark already I could barely make out shapes of trees. I'd been staring at that stupid stick so long I hadn't noticed anything else.

All of a sudden we were running, and we didn't stop until we came to the water. It was a little bit better there because it was lighter in the open, and if we looked up we could see a few hazy stars scattered around.

There was nothing else to do, so we sat down and leaned back against two trees and watched that black water moving along like the back of some big oily sea serpent.

"You reckon we'll leave our bones here?" Lonnie said.

"You mean _die?_ Like starving to death?"

"If we do, I'll bet you we come back to haint the place."

"Not me!" I said. "You can if you want to. I don't intend to hang around to haint anyplace and especially not this island."

"Haints don't get to choose where they haint. They hadn't got any sayso. They have to come back to the place that pulls them."

"Let's talk about something else, Lonnie. All right?" I said. It was getting me down, all that about haints. How long could a person go without food, anyway? I thought I might already be getting weak.

"Lonnie, what would you have to eat right this minute if you could have anything?" I said, trying to find something that would cheer us up.

"Oh, lordy. Pinto beans and cornbread. Fried chicken, all wings. Turnip greens. Homemade peach ice cream. What would you?"

"A hamburger with pickles and mustard and onions on it. French fries. Chocolate milk shake so thick you couldn't even suck it through a straw."

We both groaned, practically able to see all those things to eat just floating in the air around us. I could practically smell that hamburger. Onion and all.

My stomach let out a big growl and so did Lonnie's. It sounded like our stomachs were going to hold some kind of conversation between themselves, all complaining and whining.

"I guess we could be worse off," Lonnie said, "if it was winter."

"If it was winter, we wouldn't be here. And there wouldn't be mosquitoes, either." They'd found us, all right, zinging around our ears and biting our arms and legs and anything else they could get to.

I don't think I've ever felt as miserable before as I did then. I knew nobody was going to find us before morning, and we were going to be there the whole night in the dark being hungry and chewed by mosquitoes. I knew how worried Mom and Grandma must be, and there wasn't anything I could do about it. If I'd been by myself I'd have cried. I'd have howled the way Geronimo did that night I stayed at Lonnie's house. As it was my eyes got kind of wet.

"Maybe we ought to try to make ourselves beds the ways dogs do," Lonnie said. "You know, when they scratch with their paws and dig them out a place."

We didn't have anything to lose so we tried it in the sand, scooping it out until we had two shallow trenches we could lie down in. We put little piles of sand for pillows and tried them out. We had to lie straight on our backs because we hadn't made the trenches very wide, and we used the extra sand to cover ourselves over in order to discourage the mosquitoes. It wasn't exactly comfortable, but it was better than nothing.

We lay there looking up at the sky.

"Know what it feels like I'm lying in?" Lonnie said.

"Yeah, but don't say it." I'd had the very same thought — there we were stretched out on our backs like dead people in their coffins.

I tried to pretend that I was on that island where Ned and his friends camped, and that Ned was over on the other side, but it didn't work very well. Then I told myself that Lonnie and I were Tarantula and the Red Chigger, after all, and we could get out of this anytime we wanted to if we used our super-powers. But that didn't work very well either.

"You asleep, Lonnie?"

"Nope."

"You going to sleep?"

"Nope."

"You staying awake all night?"

"Yep."

"So am I."

I didn't, though, because I woke up in the middle of the night when it started thundering.

# Chapter

## 10

"Lonnie!" I said, shaking him by the shoulder. "You hear that, Lonnie?"

Lonnie rolled over on his side, and I could tell he was listening too.

"Isn't that thunder?" I said, although I knew perfectly well it was.

"Sure, it's thunder."

"Well, what're we going to do?"

"How do I know?" Lonnie said, sounding cross.

Right then there was a streak of lightning in the west and behind it a big rumble of thunder.

It was still hot where we were. Not a breath of wind stirring.

"I don't know about you," I said, "but I'm going to try to find something to get under."

There wasn't even a leaf to crawl under on the beach, so I ran for the trees in the middle of the island.

"Worst place is in under trees," Lonnie said, running along at my elbow.

"Not as bad as being out there on the beach," I shouted back at him.

When the flashes of lightning came they lit everything up with a peculiar-looking purple light, and we could see the trees and bushes and even the path, but between flashes it was dark and we had to stumble along by feel. By the time we got to the circle of rocks, the wind had started and there were fat drops of rain in it.

"This way," Lonnie said, pulling me through the bushes. In the next lightning flash I saw a big cedar tree with its branches reaching down to the ground. "Get in under here," Lonnie said, so I crawled behind him between the branches as best I could. Right against the tree trunk there was a little space where we could almost sit up, but that's all you could say for the place. There were spiderwebs all over. They got on my cheeks and in my hair, and when we leaned against the tree trunk, we got sticky stuff from the bark on our shirts. We weren't even safe from the rain. When it came, it came in a heavy sheet washing through those cedar branches like they weren't even there.

"Another one of your smart ideas, Lonnie," I said.

He was too miserable to answer me back. We sat huddled with our knees under our chins and leaned together to keep warm, but that rain pounded in on us and soaked even our sneakers. Water ran down the back of my neck and dripped off my hair.

It didn't rain long, but it was even worse somehow when the rain stopped. There we were, wet to the skin and cold, in a night dark as pitch, with nowhere we could move that would be any better. We just sat there shivering with our heads on our knees.

"Make like we've got this great big fire going, and we're sitting right by it, and it's all hot on our faces and our arms and everything," Lonnie said. "Can't you pretty near feel it?"

"No, I can't," I said. "I can't imagine any fire, and I don't want to imagine what I'd eat for breakfast if I was home, either. I don't want to imagine anything."

"OK," Lonnie said, "but that fire sure feels good."

I'd have kicked him in the shin only I didn't want to uncurl from my ball.

I didn't exactly go to sleep, but I had a dream, anyway. Something about sliding down a snow-covered mountainside, grabbing at little bushes as I passed but not able to get hold of anything.

When I opened my eyes again, it was getting to be daylight. The sky was clear overhead and the birds were singing. I was damp, but I wasn't soaking and the air was warm. I was all prickly, though, where the rain had dried on me. When I moved my head a cascade of raindrops came down on my head from the cedar branches, and I knew I didn't want to spend the rest of the day under there.

"Lonnie!" I said, nudging him in the ribs. "Pancakes and maple syrup!"

Lonnie jerked his head up and his nose started sniffing like a rabbit's.

"I really got you that time," I said. "You could just see those pancakes floating around in the air, couldn't you?"

"I was sound asleep," Lonnie said, sounding mad. "I won't let you get by with that." He chased me from under the tree and we ran all the way across the island two times before I let him catch me. I flopped down in the sand and let him give me a couple of punches on the shoulder, which was only fair.

"Let's pull off everything and get dry," he said, so we did that. We put our shorts and shirts and our underwear out on some rocks by the water so the sun could get to them, and we ran in the sand getting slowly dried out and warm. The sun had just come up — it was five-thirty — but it already had some heat in it. You could feel it warm on your skin. At home the air would've been cool and the dew heavy and chilly on the grass.

We felt good after we'd been running awhile, or at least we felt warm; the heat didn't do a thing for our other problems.

"My stomach's thin as a dime," Lonnie said.

When we sucked our stomachs in we could get our hands practically all the way around our waists. "We're shrinking up," Lonnie said. "We can't last another day out here."

Anything would be better than another day out there on the island without anything to eat.

"I don't know about you, but I'm ready to swim for it," Lonnie said.

I'd been looking at the water myself with the very same thought in my head. The water looked a lot friendlier than it had the night before. The sun was shining on it, and it was bright and glittered like something you could pick up in your hands. The current was so quiet you had to look hard to see that the water was moving along.

"Don't you think we ought to wait awhile, though?" I said. "Somebody's bound to come along this morning."

"You can hang around here starving to death if you want to, but I'm going back," Lonnie said. "When I get home I'll tell them where you are and some-body'll come after you."

He took his shorts off the rock where they'd been drying and started putting them on.

"Listen here, Lonnie," I said, really getting mad at him, "don't you act so smart with me. You know you can't swim worth a darn, and if you start out by yourself, you'll probably drown out there in the middle."

"I will not! And if I do, what'll it be to you? I'd rather drown than sit around here all day."

He meant it too. If it had been Richard, now, instead of Lonnie, I'd have known that he'd back down at the last minute. He might walk right down to the water and even wade in an inch or two, but then he'd stop and say, "Don't you think, whatever we do, we better stick together, Ben?" and then he'd stand there waiting for me to say sure we ought to stick together, and we ought to wait awhile before setting out.

But with Lonnie it was different. Once he set his jaw in that stubborn, Red Chigger way he'd go on and do whatever it was if it killed him. If he knew for sure he was going to sink like a rock before he could get to the other side of the river, he'd set out just the same.

If I hadn't let Lonnie talk me into taking the rowboat we wouldn't be in this mess. I should have just started walking the other way when he began talking, but I didn't do it. Don't ask me why I always end up listening to Lonnie. But it seems like there's always some good reason. Take this situation right here, for example. I couldn't just sit watching Lonnie trying to get across that river when all he can do is dog paddle. I wasn't about to have to tell his mother that he'd drowned out there and I hadn't gone with him, even though I'm five times the swimmer he is.

"When we get to the other side I'm going to kill

you, Lonnie, so it's not going to do you any good to get across," I said to him, reaching for my shorts.

He just grinned and danced around on his toes like a boxer working out.

"We'll be home by breakfast time, Tarantula, and shoot, you'll be biting into sausage and egg before you can say turnip greens." Good old Lonnie — all full of enthusiasm.

I didn't feel very good about it myself. In fact, I felt uneasy. When I took off my watch and put it in one of my sneakers I had a sudden picture of Mom and Dad and Ned seeing that little heap of things lying there after I drowned. The neatness would make them cry. I'm not ordinarily that neat.

Lonnie ran past me and jumped out into the water.

"What's it like?" I yelled when he came up.

"Wettest thing you ever jumped in. Not a bit cold."

I jumped in too, and I saw he was right. It felt kind of cold when you first hit the water, but by the time you surfaced you were pretty much used to it. And that current, why, that current was great! It was sort of boosting us along to where we wanted to go anyway. We could've just floated on our backs and it probably would have brought us to that spit of land just before the river makes its turn. Just at the place we turned Wol loose.

"Boy, this is fun!" I shouted to Lonnie. "Why

didn't we do this yesterday afternoon? We were crazy."

For some reason it made me want to laugh when I thought about us starving on the island and getting rained on when, if we'd just used our gumption, as Lonnie would say, we could have gotten ourselves out of that mess as easy as pie.

"Shoot, we're already halfway there," Lonnie said, his head sticking out of the water like a turtle's. He was chugging along like a turtle, too, not very fast but steady.

"I can't *wait* to get home, can you? Running up that road yelling and carrying on."

I was just opening my mouth to say something when all of a sudden a pain shot through my leg. I kept trying to kick, but the pain got worse and then I was sinking like a rock, my mouth filling with water. It took me a few seconds to understand what was happening, because it had never happened to me before. When my head came up to the surface I yelled "Cramp!" at Lonnie before I went down again.

I don't know what I thought Lonnie could do since he wasn't much good at keeping even himself afloat, much less somebody else, but there wasn't anybody else to yell to.

I went down in the water again. The water deep in the river was cold and murky, and this time it didn't seem like I would come up. My lungs were burning; I was strangling. I thought I was going to die.

The water turned me around and around and there was a rushing noise in my ears. Somehow, without knowing I was doing it, I managed to use my arms to get to the surface, and the sun, when I opened my eyes and saw it, was the sweetest thing I'd ever seen.

When I felt myself sinking again I really panicked, but somehow Lonnie managed to take my arm.

"Hang on," he yelled, so I grabbed him around the waist and held on while we both sank.

When we came up again, I was still hanging on to Lonnie, and he started dog paddling furiously. I could feel through the muscles in his back how hard he was working. He was sunk in the water right up to his chin, but that didn't keep him from trying. I stayed low in the water, the pain in my leg so bad I couldn't do much.

"You can't make it," I yelled to Lonnie. "It's too far."

"Shut up and hang on," Lonnie said, between breaths. He was already breathing like a winded horse, and we still had quite a way to go. I could see the trees on the bank, but it was like another country over there. One we'd never get to.

I could see that our only hope was that the current would take us close enough to the bank when we went by the point so that we could somehow get to shore from there.

"Bank," I said to Lonnie when I came up for air. He didn't bother to nod, but I knew he understood.

"Just . . . hang . . . on," he said, his voice sounding funny.

I had to hand it to him — he was stubborn.

We were coming up to the point now, and I could feel Lonnie giving it all he had, trying to work us over to the shore. I saw, too, that we weren't going to make it. We were going to miss by about fifty feet, and although that may not sound like much, it was going to be enough. I couldn't get through fifty feet of water myself, still doubled up with the cramp, and Lonnie didn't have the strength to pull us out of the current and through those fifty feet by himself.

We came up even with the point. I've never seen in my life anything more clearly than I saw a willow tree growing by the water, and an old half-rotted log jammed against the bank. I could see orange lichen growing on the log, and the long, skinny, silvery green leaves of the willow tree — every one of them, it seemed like.

Then we were past the point; I could see the river opening out again, and I knew it was all over. Lonnie couldn't hold out more than a few more minutes, and from now on we were getting farther from the shore all the time. I knew we were going to drown, yet I wasn't exactly scared. Maybe I was too tired to be scared. I'd heard that when people are about to drown they see their whole lives go by like in a movie. I didn't see anything like that — not my whole life, anyway. What I did see was Mom, Dad, Ned, and me sitting at the dinner table at home, and Ned and I were tickling each other under the table — one of us was going to give way any second and laugh like crazy and have to leave the table. That seemed to me a really odd thing to remember when I expected to drown any minute.

All of a sudden I guess Lonnie's legs and arms just gave out, because we were both under the water, and all I could see was arms and legs churning around and brown water, and somehow there seemed to be a lot of noise, although I didn't think I was making any myself.

Then I came to the surface and saw where the noise was coming from — the best sight I've ever seen in my life. There was Myra, shouting and swimming out to us holding a long stick, pushing it through the water. "Hold on!" she was yelling. "Come here!" I grabbed Lonnie again before I could sink, and he managed to get us both over to Myra and her stick. I grabbed one end and he grabbed the other, and Myra kicked and breathed, kicked and breathed, until she got us to the shore.

I don't have much memory of getting out of the water and flopping down on the beach. But after I'd been lying there for what seemed like a long time just getting my breath back, I opened my eyes and right there was the sky — pale and light like the inside of an eggshell — and the leaves just waving a little over my head. I was so happy just to see those things and know I was alive that I wanted to yell and run around in circles, only I didn't have the strength. I felt then that I'd be happy the rest of my life just having the sky and the trees to look at.

"Hey, Lonnie, I bet I drank half that river," I said to him.

"Naw, you didn't. I did." He lifted himself on one elbow and gave me that funny grin of his. "Who's the best swimmer now, huh, you or me?"

"I guess it has to be you, Red Chigger," I said.

"You're darn right it's me," Lonnie said. "Don't you forget it, either, Tarantula."

I felt like kicking him back into the river, even if he had saved my life.

# Chapter

## 11

"**B**oys, we've got to get up to the house and telephone your mothers right away," Myra said. "Everybody thinks you're dead. Drowned."

"They didn't even know we were out there in the river," I said. "Why should they think we were drowned?"

"Because somebody found my boat overturned in the river under the Sherburn bridge, and since you were both missing, everybody assumed you'd taken the boat out on the river, upturned it, and drowned. People have been up and down the river banks all night, hoping you might have managed to swim ashore, but as time went on that seemed less and less likely. We knew that Lonnie wasn't a very good swimmer, so by daylight, when nobody had heard anything out of you, we thought you'd drowned."

Lonnie cleared his throat self-importantly. "I

was the one got us across the river. Ben got a cramp and I had to do everything."

"We'd still have drowned if Myra hadn't come out after us," I said.

"No, we wouldn't. I would've got us on across. All I needed was just to catch my breath."

"While you were catching your breath we would've drowned."

"You sure are a fine one to talk! You'd be right at the bottom of the river right now if I hadn't . . ."

"Boys, help me up," Myra interrupted, holding out her hands to us. "I can't even get myself off the ground in these soaking clothes. You both did remarkably well, and Lonnie came up trumps, seems to me. I saw how hard you were struggling out there, Lonnie."

Well, it was true. It was just his bragging I didn't like.

We pulled Myra to her feet and she put on her boots, which she'd left on shore, and we started up the bank. "Now tell me the whole story," Myra said. "About the boat and why it was so far downstream when you were up here."

So we did. About seeing Wol and about the Mannings taking the boat and the thunderstorm and everything. Myra got very indignant about the Mannings and said it was one thing to play a little harmless trick on somebody and another to go to the lengths they had — upturning the boat in a place where it was bound to be seen and letting everyone draw the obvious conclusion. Giving everybody worry and grief and having no telling how many people would spend the night going up and down the riverbank with flashlights. Even the National Guard had come out to look for us and would have started dragging the river this morning. In fact, the helicopter we'd seen flying over the island late the afternoon before had been heading down the river to look for us. Nobody had supposed that we could have been so far upriver as the island.

"Why were you looking for us here this morning?" I asked Myra, who was walking bowlegged because of all the water in her jeans.

"To tell you the truth, I wasn't looking for you exactly. I'd spent the night at your grandmother's house making coffee and coordinating the search so people were covering as much ground as possible. But at daylight I decided to come home for a while and gather my strength again. For me there's no better way to gather my strength than to go out at daylight looking for birds. It was by chance that I came to the river, although that's often the place I do go. I was looking for herons when I saw your heads bobbing around in the water."

"How did you know it was us?" I asked.

"Who else could it have been? I kicked off my boots, grabbed the pole I use to push the boat off in the water, and ran. 'Myra, my girl,' I kept saying to myself, 'you're too old to do this sort of thing, but you're going to have to do it anyway even if you die in the attempt.' "

"Boy, I sure would like to get my hands on those Mannings," Lonnie said. "I'd fry 'em in oil, I sure would. Going hungry and getting rained on and practically drowning. How would they like that?"

Myra telephoned Grandma's house as soon as we got up the hill. She stood dripping all over the floor while she shouted into the telephone that she'd found us and we were alive and not even hurt. Then I talked to my mother, whose voice sounded kind of watery, and Lonnie talked to his mother, who was at Grandma's house, too, while Myra changed out of her wet clothes.

Then she drove us home.

Home was a shock. Even before we got to Grandma's house we saw cars and trucks parked along the side of the road and along the driveway, and I could tell from a distance that Grandma's yard was full of people.

"What's going on?" I said. "What're all these people doing here?"

"They just want to see you two alive and well. Some of these people have been out all night looking for you."

Suddenly I felt shy, seeing all those people waiting for us, but Lonnie perked up and got excited. He put his head out the window and started waving. It's funny how different things make different people feel shy.

"There're even soldiers!" Lonnie said. "And there's Jesse sitting on the porch steps spitting tobacco juice in your grandma's four o'clocks."

"I see him," I said, sliding down in the seat.

As soon as I got out of the car, Mom grabbed me and hugged me, and Grandma hugged me, and then people I didn't even know grabbed me and hugged me, and Jesse was saying, "We thought you young 'uns were goners for sure."

Lonnie's whole family was there too, including Sylvie and Geronimo. People kept looking at us expectantly like they were waiting for us to do something unusual. I couldn't think of anything, but Lonnie wasn't bothered. He started telling anybody who cared to listen about how he'd saved my life. That's what people wanted to hear, I guess, because a lot of them crowded around him to listen.

After a few minutes, though, Myra called out in a loud voice, "These boys must be famished. Don't you think we ought to get something solid inside them?"

That broke up the party, more or less. Lonnie went off with his family, and I went into the kitchen with Mom and Grandma, and everybody else started drifting away too.

"Guess what?" Mom said, giving me another

hug and kiss in the kitchen. "We have to go out to the airport at twelve to collect your father."

"You mean, Dad's coming?"

"He's leaving his workshop a week early. I telephoned him last night, of course, when we were so worried about you, and he made plans then to leave. I telephoned him again this morning as soon as Myra let us know that you were all right, but he said he'd come on anyway. Now we'll all drive home together. Won't that be nice?"

"When'll we leave?"

"Three or four days, I guess."

I wanted to see Dad, of course — that was good. But I wasn't enthusiastic about leaving so soon, not when things were just getting good.

Grandma cooked a big breakfast of fried ham and grits and eggs and biscuits. I really dug in, but I didn't eat as much as I thought I would when we were on the island. I got full quickly and couldn't eat another bite. Maybe my stomach had shrunk and couldn't hold as much as it used to.

It was great meeting Dad at the airport. He looked just the same, only he was browner than he had been, and he was wearing a new shirt. He brought me a shell he'd found on a beach and a superhero mobile that I could hang above my bed when we got home. I'd be able to watch Spiderman and Captain America and the Silver Surfer flying around over my head in a breeze.

Somehow, with Dad around, I didn't see much of my friends, but on the next to last day we were there, he took me into town to buy presents for everybody. Jesse was easy. I got him a can of Prince Albert and that was all right. And I picked out a white china hen for Grandma. The hen lifted off a nest that you could put things in. It took me a while to find something for Myra. It seemed to me she already had everything. I ended up getting a straw hat with a wide, floppy brim and a blue ribbon around the crown. I got a box of raisins for Willie, too. Dad noticed that I wasn't getting anything for Lonnie, but I said that was all right. I had something better for him than anything I could buy there.

I think Myra liked the hat. She said that she didn't know why she hadn't thought of buying one before — the helmet wasn't right for Arkansas, as she should have realized long before. She had a present for me, too. It was a picture of a screech owl in a frame. I could hang it up in my room, she said, to remind me of Wol. She also gave one to Lonnie. I liked it, but the owl in the picture wasn't as pretty as Wol was. It was just any old screech owl, and Wol wasn't like any other one.

I know Willie liked the raisins, because he opened the box and had most of them eaten by the time I left the house.

Jesse was asleep on his cot when I came to give him the Prince Albert, but I woke him up. He said he'd be back next summer, same as always, and he'd take Lonnie and me fishing to a special place he knows about.

It was hardest telling Lonnie good-bye. I went over to his house late in the afternoon, and he was sitting on the front porch with Sylvie. He didn't come out to meet me the way he usually did, and I knew he hated it too — saying good-bye. It made us feel, somehow, the way we had that first day in the tree house before we got to know each other. I sat down on the step beside him, and we didn't say anything. Sylvie climbed in my lap, but I didn't mind. Babies aren't so bad once you get to know them.

"What's up, Lonnie?" I asked.

"Nothing much. What's up with you?"

"Brought you something," I said, and handed him over a paper sack that had all my comics in it, even the old ones.

"You don't have to give me anything," he said, starting to get on his high horse.

"I want you to keep them for me," I said. "You can have them and read them all winter, but they're still officially mine."

"What if the mice get to them?"

"You better put them someplace safe. These are my very best comics, the real old ones, and if you let anything happen to them I'll kill you when I come back next summer."

Lonnie looked a lot more cheerful. "You and

who else?" he said. "Say, I got something for you too. I just remembered." He ran into the house to get whatever it was, and I was left with Sylvie in my lap. I'd brought her a little truck that had belonged to Ned and me before we pretty much outgrew trucks. I didn't know if she'd like it or not, but when I took it from behind my back and held it out, she grabbed it and chuckled. Then she got out of my lap to try it out on the porch, and I crawled around with her making truck noises. In no time she was making truck noises too. That's one of the things about little kids. It's fun to teach them things. Like with a parrot, I guess, only little kids pick things up faster than a parrot.

Lonnie came back with a Mason jar and something silvery inside. Something rolled up around and around. Lonnie opened the jar and started pulling the silvery thing out very carefully, and I saw it was a snake skin. A whopper. We stretched it across the porch and it was six feet at least.

"This is the best one I ever did find," Lonnie said, "and it's got even the head and tail. Snake skins tear up easy, though, so you'll have to watch out for it."

"Nobody at home will have seen a snake skin like this one. I'll be real careful, Lonnie, and bring it back next summer."

Well, that was all settled and there didn't seem much more to say. Lonnie and Sylvie walked with me down to the road, and Lonnie held Sylvie up so she could wave bye.

"Bye," she said, waving like crazy. "Bye, bye. Bye, Ben."

"Hey, did you hear that?" I shouted to Lonnie. "She said 'Ben.' She's learned my name."

"Sure," Lonnie said.

I kept waving as long as I could see the two of them, and every time Sylvie waved back.

The day after we got back home I wrote Lonnie a letter. I told him about seeing a house on fire going through St. Louis and about finding a dime in a pay phone in the Holiday Inn in Effingham, Illinois, and what Richard had said when he saw the snake skin. Which was, "Don't touch me with that thing." I said that Ned was kind of envious of the water-witching stick and made me try it out in our yard. It wouldn't work there — maybe there's no water under our yard or maybe I needed a greener stick — but I faked it and half-fooled him anyway.

I didn't know if Lonnie would write back or not, but he did, right away. A snapping turtle had bitten him on the finger and it was all swollen up, and everybody had made such a fuss about the Manning boys and what they had done that their daddy had decided they were going to have to shape up and had sent them off to their uncle in Texas, who had a wheat farm. Leroy and Butchie were going to work in the wheat harvest and stay on out there if they made good hands. "I hope it's a hundert degrees in the shade and the wheat fuzz gets all down their backs and drives them crazy, don't you?" Lonnie wrote.

I said I hoped so too. I hoped they'd stay the rest of their lives out there boiling their brains — what they had of them.

To tell the truth, though, I wouldn't care too much if they were back again in Arkansas in the summer. It wouldn't be quite the same without them. We needed villains, Tarantula and the Red Chigger did. After all, a superhero is just a person wearing a silly suit, without villains to overcome.